I0621200

Message from the High Inquest
A Schism with Rome

In this issue of *Inquestor Tales*, I'm reprinting the story that began the whole series — and it's the original version that became non-canonical by the inclusion of a single Latin phrase:

pater noster qui es in inferno

You see, the story that set all this in motion was a one-off.   Indeed, it had something to do with a big rollercoaster somewhere near Richmond, Virginia, in an amusement part called King's Dominion. It was about a 90 minute drive from Alexandria, Virginia-not-Egypt, and I would often go there to let off steam.   The rollercoaster was called *Rebel Yell* and I was younger then, I used to love rollercoasters, indeed I collected them.

I wasn't sure whether I would even call them *Inquestors*. My first thought was that there would be a clear line of succession from the inquistion and thus they would have to be inquisitors.   Since this was a 12,000 word novelette, not a five-book series with thousands of pages of backstory and language notes, and since science fiction is supposed to be *show, don't tell,* dropping a misquote from the Lord's Prayer was the fastest way to provide a few millennia of speculative backstory to the character of Ton Davaryush.

So, the original story, *The Thirteenth Utopia,* was at first tethered to the history of the Roman Catholic Church, with the reader's images of the Inquisition providing context to its events.

However, the tale, as Tolkien would put it, "grew in the telling." It didn't just grow in one direction. *The Thirteenth Utopia* was not the beginning, nor even the middle, or the end. It was a snapshot from somewhere in a massive continuum that was slowly coming into focus, a piece here, a piece there. Even now, forty years after the *The Thirteenth Utopia* came out, more fragments are emerging. Like the fact that there was more than one Sajit.

(Sajit — the poetic voice of a million worlds and twenty millennia — well, how could he be *other* than a multi-body person? But that is a different essay.)

As the Inquestor universe grew into its past as well as its future, it became clear that it needed to be unmoored from Earth.

My choice to deviate from the term *inquisitor* and to invent a new word proved to be liberating. (And odd therefore that in some translations, like the French version, the High Inquest has been rendered as the Inquisition after all.)

The root word *inquest,* in any case, adds the implication of a *coroner's inquest* to the word. That the rich, lush, brilliantly colored universe laced with savagery that I created and which the Inquestors scrutinize with such ruthlessness is not only vibrantly alive, but also already dead.

And in the end Catholicism didn't seem to be the right coloration for the Inquestors. Certainly, they have *guilt* — but not in the same way. The Inquestors have the ostentation, self-righteousness and intellectual gymnastics characteristic of a certain segment of the Catholic Church especially during the periods in history when people really believed in a physical heaven — and

INQUESTOR TALES

Despatches from the High Inquest • Number Four •
February, 2020
Diplodocus Press • Bangkok • Los Angeles

Contents

ISBN: 978-1-940999-48-7
Diplodocus Press
Bangkok • Los Angeles
www.diplodocuspress.com

---

even more in a physical hell. But the Inquestors don't have a God. Or do they? That is something that may be revealed in a later novel in this endless "trilogy".

I had thought that this fourth issue of *Inquestor Tales* might see the final installment of *Homeworld of the Heart,* but there's another chunk coming.

In addition, I'm afraid, there's at least two more books, and so I will just continue to serialize as long as the story keeps flowing.

The bad news is, if you collect all the issues, you might not arrive at a final complete edition of the novel because I can already some chapters that I would like to have included. Like an early childhood memory of Sajit's involving twins and a deadly ceremony.

The Somtow completist might end up having the buy the book *and* collect the *Tales* which in any case contain ancillary materially that might not be collected elsewhere.

So please, allow me to thank all those who have continued on this journey with me. It is amazing to revisit the beginnings of my science fiction career, and more amazing still to discover that my youthful self has more stories to tell me.

It's like a time-loop story when you meet an older version of yourself who tells you things you need to know in order to grow to become that older self.

Except in this case, it's the other way round.

— Somtow

CHRONICLES OF THE HIGH INQUEST
The Homeworld of the Heart

by S.P. Somtow

Part IV
THE SPACE BETWEEN SPACES

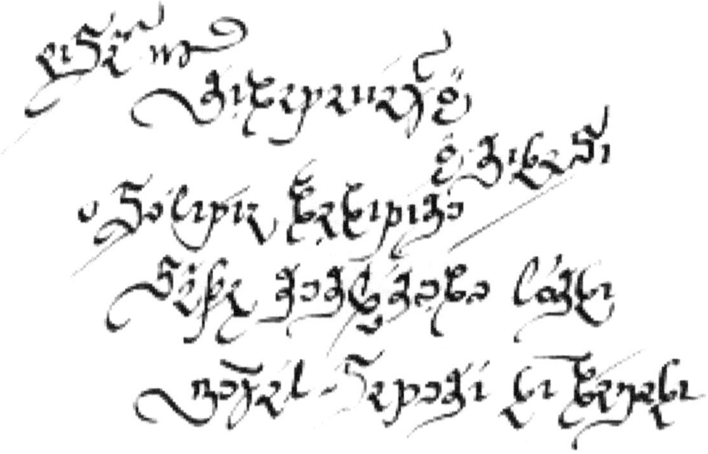

aiváh! aiváh!
kindarayághor or-kitávi
uraná vrendáh
u velirís dhandiríske
vãzhas kekýrkende lukti
meghal-vareký ti dhánati

He comes! He comes!
The child collector with his golden scroll!
He'll take you to the sky
Where you'll fly, where you'll die
spinning disks of light,
with your lightning eyes of death.

— traditional

Thirteen

Safety

Paradise lasted only a sleep or two; in the temple in the forest, Tijas and Sajit soon became hungry. There was a *gruyesh* tree, so by the second sleep they had picked all the fruit and sucked the juices dry and picked up a case of diarrhea besides.

Wandering further, they found another tree, but there is such a thing as too much sweetness.

"We should go to the house," Sajit said.

"House?"

"*Our* house."

"Except that I never lived there."

"You did. But you were in a box."

"I'm not *attached* to that place. I mean, I don't feel that it's *home.*"

"It doesn't matter. It's got food. At least, it still had food when we left home for the city."

Indeed, Sajit had been thinking of home since they arrived at the ruined temple. He wanted Tijas to love *home* as well, but perhaps it was true that he couldn't feel connected to it in the same way. But he know how to get them there. First, to the clearing, then a brief walk through the wood. Tijas was reluctant, but even he knew they couldn't live on *gruyesh* forever.

The village of Attembris was no more than the journey of a sleep. Sajit could tell the way easily, not so much by the trees and the twisted pathway, but by the scent of the rosellas, becoming more intense as they neared the ring of stones where he used to come in the night to be alone with the moons and with his music.

The petals whirled and churned.   The moons danced.

And presently, they were at the edge of the village. They stood in front of the wall to Sajit's room, which abutted the forest, was indeed almost indistinguishable from the forest, as it was cloaked in a mirroring filter that reflected and re-reflected the trees.   But the bedroom window was still keyed to Sajit's DNA; he touched a low-hanging branch and they climbed inside easily enough, though inside seemed at first to be just a continuation of outside; the holosculpt of the forest was still running.

Most would not hear it, but Sajit's fine-tuned hearing sensed the threshold thrum of a holosculptor, and he wondered why the house was still connected the the planetary thinkhive's power.

The boys were both standing in Sajit's old room now. For a moment it seemed that the last year had been a dream. Only … there were two of him now.

Sajit tapped the wall to see if there was any food. It wheezed a bit and extruded a loaf of something vaguely protein, vaguely bread. "The kitchen is sort of working," he said.   They shared the loaf; doubtless it was an admixture of all the right nutrients, but there was a staleness, as though the domestic thinkhive had become unused to cooking.

Thinkhives. They could be as cranky as people.

Tijas said, "At least it's not another gruyesh."

"Let's go to the family area," said Sajit, "perhaps there's a deactivated servocorpse we left behind, and we can kickstart it and make it turn the house into something livable."

He took his doppling's hand and they entered the breakfast circle where the family usually gathered. For the first time in months Sajit missed Vimla and Chanika. The sisters, the parents — or the people who he had thought to be his parents and his siblings — their chatter was so much a part of this room.

But yes, it had a scent of home. Perhaps a hint of a fragrance Ina sometimes wore. Perhaps the sour odor of a fermenting bowl of *zul*. Perhaps the sound of a whisperlyre —

No! "Tijas, we're not imagining this."

The first tones of an *alap*, the introduction to a song ... a love song. The choice of raga was anterior-retrograde, each tone nudged toward the flat side by a single *shrut* in the descent, as if to speak of regret, of love lost.

"Where is it coming from?" said Tijas.

And then came words:

bhasháur hyemádhen chítarans
Ga eyáh jariti
midhiá bhashandut

The boys knew that song well.

Some say that the homeworld of the heart

Is legendary Earth; though that's just a story.

They sang the next lines, coming in an improvised canon, adding florid melismata to the song's sustained tones:

*z chítarans hyemádhen bhasháur
Uran s'Vareken, hokhkeliassá*

*but others say the heart's homeworld
is the High Eye of Heaven,
where the High Compassion dwells —*

As they sang, the front door of the house irised open, and they could see a hooded, bent figure in the garden. He was looking away from them, but the knew who it was. They knew that they should be quiet, that they should not reveal themselves — not *both* of them. But they were caught up in the magic of the song.

*bhasháurke ma u ejéndut
ma kens savra bhasháh
mori, hesti, darlukti
kal flúh em flúta*

*still others that it's the planet of our birth
the world whose fragrance speaks of
mother, the hearth, the light of a star
that flows like a river*

It was the final stanza that made transformed these musings into a love song. But whether it was the love of lovers, of brothers, or of a master and student or even a human being and a world, a god, a cosmos ... that was ambiguous.

The boys sang, blending with an old man singing to himself in a light-drenched garden in a house in an abandoned village.

má bhashávo sarnang
hokhté chitres-hyémadh
midhiá em ga
em enguesta keliásek
melít em matésavra

but I say you are the heart's homeworld,
as mythical as Earth,
as compassionate as the High Inquest,
as sweet as the scent of a mother.

The music died away and it was Arbát who stood and turned to see them, the old teacher in a white robe in the entryway. The sunlight in the garden was bright and Arbát was a shadow.

Arbát said, "Don't be afraid. I hoped against hope there would be two Sajits."

The boys looked at each other, and back to their teacher.

"You're a gift to the world, to the whole Dispersal of Man, Sajit. I knew my purpose in life was to take you, the rough-edged genius, to polish, to purify, to refine ... and then to give you up, because you belong to all the cosmos. Your words, your music. I am only a servant of the Art, Sajit, and I knew you were not mine to keep.

But I always dreamed there would be a second Sajit, and that he could belong to me."

Sajit said, "We don't belong to you, Master Arbát."

Their teacher sighed. "Yes, that, also, I know." He set down the whisperlyre on the floor of the dwelling and walked over to where the boys were standing. He laid one hand on each boy's cheek. "You see, I am not horrified at the abomination. I'm not superstitious. How could I be, when I have digested the great songs of so many cultures, so many worlds?"

"But why are you in Attembris?" Tijas said.

"I thought you would come here. The city is a mess, imperfectly matched with an alien city, its sense of direction all topsy turvy. Combing through the city's grid can lead to many wrong turns; the cities are still intertwining as they begin to coexist. But Attembris may as well not exist at all."

"But what will we do?" Tijas said.

"You'll be safe here, Sajit."

"I'm not Sajit. I'm Tijas."

This comment seemed to pass unnoticed. Sajit could not fail to see how Tijas felt about it. Tijas was not another Sajit. Tijas was Tijas and Sajit, chronologically older, felt it was up to him to insist on it. "Master Arbát," he said, "you have to understand. You've been teaching us both, but you never knew which was which."

"Why does it matter? The spirit of music has granted my heart's desire. I can keep you with me always, *and* I can let you go."

"No, we're not the same person."

So Sajit understood that much as Arbát may have wanted to protect him, there was also something not quite right about this relationship.   There was an obsessiveness.   Why else would the old man come to Attembris? Why would he *stalk* them?

Arbát said, "I've filled the house with supplies ... got them from other houses in the village.   The place is almost completely deserted."

"Almost?" Tijas said.

"There are a few families ... families so uninvolved in the world that they hardly even understand that our planet has *fallen beyond.* Some of them are living in the school. You remember it, Sajit."

"Tijas."

Sajit thought, *Why does he always look at Tijas and say* Sajit? *Why, when he can't even tell us apart?*

Tijas looked at him as if Sajit had spoken aloud. He must have divined his thoughts. He whispered in Sajit's ear, "It's because I was the one who ... caught him with the pleasure corpse. He senses that."

***

Gharém emerged, at least, from his dungeon.   He assumed Mikkálu would be waiting around in an antechamber, but there was no one. Only an attendant, dozing on a cushion of force.

Enraged, Gharém shook the man.

"You've finished, my Lord," he said.   "I hope our service was satisfactory."

"Where is my equerry?"

"He went to pray to the goddess, my Lord."

"Tell him we are going back to work."

"Oh ... no, my Lord. We never disturb the goddess."

"What do you mean? This whorehouse is infested with two-gipfer goddesses. Surely my servant may be pulled away from whatever depraved thing he's doing."

"Oh ... your equerry is not engaged in any recreational activities, sir. He's not just with one of our priestesses who assumes the role of Aërat. He is with Aërat herself. They were friends, you know, before he joined the childsoldiers. Friends as children."

"That means nothing. A childsoldier has no past."

"And yet, Lord, if you are in no hurry ... perhaps another visit to our dungeons?"

Gharém was sated. He had tormented the dead for many sleeps. He had drenched himself in blood, semen, piss, and every foul fluid that could ooze from a corpse. "Another episode will deplete me permanently," he said.

He touched his temple with an index finger, awakening an embedded thinkhive, and subvoked a few terse commands. He saw then that Mikkálu had summoned a finding bird.

"Sneaky little squirt!" he murmured as the internal thinkhive showed him the identity of the one Mikkálu was going after. The child was going to net him the greatest prize of this haul, a childsoldier of royal blood. It was right to bring him to this world The boy *knew* things.

A childsoldier has no past, and yet ...

The Dispersal of Man is built on a foundation of equality. The Inquestors are like gods, but the humblest childsoldier could be raised to the High Inquest. And childsoldiery was the great leveller, for it was the destiny of every perfect child, lowly or noble, to serve the High Inquest and the dark game called *makrúgh*.

Mikkálu was clearly aiming to go far. He had wangled himself into Gharém's inner circle, knew Gharém's secret desires, and was, indeed, trusted by Gharém, insofar as he believed anyone could be trusted.

I will loosen the leash, Gharém thought. *Mikkálu will bring me the heir of Urna. He'll turn him over to me for ... what? a position, a commandership, something that doesn't bring death-risk with every assignment. And I will turn the child in for something big. Perhaps I shall be made a Princeling myself.*

Although then again, the High Inquest was too exalted to pay heed to the distinction between a princeling and a pauper. It was Gharém's own little game — exalting the lowly, humbling the high. *I should have been an Inquestor,* he thought. I *could* have been! If only I had not failed the compassion test.

Gharém pulled a message disk from his robe and tapped it to send a command.

Release more birds, he subvocalized, *and ready the transport. We're ready to collect the children of Urna.*
***

Orifec said, "There's something you must know about our child."

Éluma said, "I already know far more than you about our child."

"Yes. I've been distracted. But what I meant to tell you...."

The floater that had been a veranda of the princely palace moved through the night. Above them, the finding-bird wheeled, emitting its metallic-banshee screech. Mikkálu stood at the floater's edge, his slight form striated by the light from three moons, steering them, communicating with the finding bird.

But Éluma did not respond. She was always troubled now, and Orifec found her more remote. The knowledge of the dopplings was a hard, knotty thing in the back of his mind, always present. Only a member of the royal family could understand that this abomination was no abomination at all, but a different way to be human.

Orifec went to where the young equerry was steering the floater. He was flying with his eyes closed, seeing with the *veznávik's* attenuated senses.

"You saved her once," he said. "You love her, don't you?"

"You would say, I love as a child loves. And I would say to you, but you love as a princeling loves. And that can never be as deep as how a child loves."

Orifec wanted to tell him how untrue that was, how unfair ... but he doubted himself.

***

It did not feel right for the two of them to go down the school at the same time. "But," Tijas said, "we can get away with it ... if we're very sneaky."

"If some families are living there," said Sajit, "they'll have some food that's less boring than what Arbát has stashed in our walls."

And so it was that, making sure they wore an identical color of clingfire held together by the same synthserpentine belt, they made their way separately to the building where some of the families were living.

"You must not be seen together," Arbát had told them. "These are the most hidebound of all, these people. They seem rational until something cries *abomination* to them."

So that morning, Sajit entered the school and Tijas lingered outside. And Arbát sat by the door, working on a twisted new melisma for an old folk song.

Sajit only vaguely remembered these people — Tijas did not know them at all, of course. Sajit was inside, sharing a grilled heptopus and a loaf of fresh winebread with two old women. Tijas was outside and playing with other children.

Tijas had indeed not experienced a time so normal-seeming, so domestic. There was a boy named Bardelár, perhaps his age, who knew nothing about music at all, and not one word of the highspeech. But he knew all about hitting a grav-ball with a curved sick. He made the ball whir as he twirled the stick, sent it flying, swerving, almost crashing against the wall. A girl named Sávezh, his sister perhaps, was playing with a homunculus. An old dead lady, their nanny, watched them from afar.

Further away, towards the area's only displacement plate, three older children were giggling as they indulged in a three-way wrestling match.

"Want to try?" said Bardelár, throwing the stick at Tijas who caught it deftly, tried waving it a few times — it was a primitive kind of control with simple monosyllabic subvokes — *dha, dho, gha* —

The grav-ball danced in the air for a moment, defying the pull of the world —

And crashed!

Bardelár laughed as he snatched back the stick and with a wrist-flick reversed its polarity. The grav-ball swung upward.

"Stop showing off, Bardi," said his sister, before returning to snuggling with the homunculus, who bleated in a strange parody of a baby's cry.

Then it came —

A high-pitched, metallic keening first, a shriek from above, earsplitting long before its source could be seen ... it was a bird. No, not a bird. It grew closer. Bigger. Shinier, with wings that could lock position in a swooping straight streak of iridium. And when they flapped it was a sound of thunder.

Already! Tijas thought. *It only took this long to find us!*

The other children did not seem to realize there was danger. They all clustered together now, pointing, laughing, imitating the shrieking. As the bird drew closer they could see it was huge. Tijas was transfixed. *This is it, this is the end.* He reached out with his mind, trying to reach Sajit inside the school.

Adults were coming out now, but not Sajit. Tijas did not dare go inside for fear of causing an abomination panic, did not dare stay for fear of being swooped down upon, so he just stood, staring at the sky as the *veznávik* circled ever closer.

It plummeted now, diving down towards him. He screamed and —

The bird had seized the other boy.

Sávezh was shrieking. The bird's talons linked an locked to form a seat, scooping up Bardelár, knocking the grav-stick to the flagstones. The grav-ball ricocheted against the bird's skin with a clang. The linked talons extruded a restraining belt and held the terrified boy down.

"What's happening to him?" the servocorpse nanny muttered, its programming not anticipating the situation and making it walk in circles.

Then the bird flew up to the roof above the school building and spoke, it's voice chiming yet threatening, soothing yet a metallic rasp:

Glory to the High Compassion!

This child has been preordained since birth to serve the High Inquest as a childsoldier, the most glorious of all occupations. For childsoldiery is the straightest path toward receiving a clan-name and becoming more than an earthbound person. It is the path to the stars.

Parents, rejoice!

If your child survives, he will doubtless be someone of quality, someone with a true profession, someone whose clan will nurture and support for the rest of his life.

If your child falls, it is in the name of the High Compassion, which holds together the balance of the Dispersal of Man and on which all your lives depend.

Your child is a hero!

It did not seem that way to the parents, who had emerged from the building and were weeping, or to the sister who had cast the homunculus on the ground in a passion, breaking it in two, so that it squealed and begged to be glued back together, its torso walking on its arms and chasing its legs.

"Bardi! Bardi!" the parents cried. Others did too, relatives, perhaps, or friends. And Bardelár was whimpering. He had not been taught what an honour it was to have been chosen.

But presently the bird covered the boy's face with one wing, and pointed the other skyward. With a final screech it launched itself in the direction of the lowering sun.

***

At the house, Tijas said to Arbát, "You were wrong, Master Arbát. It is not safe here."

Sajit said, "We were told of the finding-birds. Each one is keyed to one child's DNA. There is one looking for us now."

"So there is nowhere on this planet you can flee to," Arbát said.

"On another planet, perhaps," Tijas said, thinking of how he had refused to go with the theater troupe.

"Urna is a backworld," Arbát said. "Now it is not even a world, because it has been folded into Alykh. Beyond this continent, there are oceans, there is another continent, we don't even know it. All we know is the star traffic."

"It will not work," said Sajit.

"We'll sleep on it," Tijas said. "Tomorrow we'll decide what to do."

***

But they did not sleep, not right away. They went to Sajit's room, opaqued the walls and the windows, made a hideaway, sealed themselves into a world.

Sajit said, "I wish —"

And Tijas knew what it was he wished for.

"There's no displacement plate here. And we can never reproduce ... the conditions."

"That place in the space between spaces," Sajit said, "that place that was a nothing expanded into realtime ... we were happy. We were inside each other's souls, completely."

No sooner had he said it than they were there again.

What? We can do this without *the displacement? How?*

They could not tell which of them was speaking.

Such a melding! Such a flooding of unknown memories! Such smells, such colors, their shared experiences made more intense by redoubled senses, overwhelming, ineffable ...

Sajittijas!!

And it was over. It had lasted ... no time at all. And like the addiction of dreamstuff, it left behind a longing, an unfulfillable need.

And they were in the room, in the darkness. Hugging one another close, in a desperate attempt to recapture the oneness.

"We can't stay," Sajit said. "And we don't have anywhere to go."

"Don't worry," Tijas said.

And he thought, *No, you shouldn't worry. I was created to worry for you. I was made to go where you should not go. I'm the spare.*

"You're *not!*" Sajit said.

And Tijas realized he had to shield his thoughts better. This connection could not be controlled. The barrier between them was weak, and not predictable.

Tijas tried to force himself to stay awake. Surely if

Sajit slept, he would be free to think some of the thoughts Sajit should not hear.

Such as what he would have to do ... to save Sajit from being found.

"Don't even think about it," Sajit said, and drifted into slumber.

Fourteen
Running Away

When Sajit awoke, Tijas was gone.

He felt the emptiness before he was even fully conscious. It was the same emptiness he'd felt in the city, when they were apart.

The Star of Urna had not even risen. Sajit deopaqued his wall and saw into the forest ... saw flattened grass patches that were perhaps footprints.

When he went to the living area he saw that Arbát was up, sitting, quite still. Sajit said, "You helped him, didn't you?"

Arbát said, "If you are separated, and you stay concealed, the finding-bird will be unable to follow you. It can't see through everything or penetrate past walls of force ... can it? And it isn't programmed to seek out ... *twins.*"

He could hardly bring himself to say the word. Even
he, who seemed to have accepted the duality, the
reasons behind it. *The idea of a doppling nauseated
him, deep down.* Sajit sensed it, and it made him
queasy.

"Where did you send him?"

"How should I know?"

"But you let him go. You've got to know where he
went."

"Far. Far."

"What kind of an answer is that?"

"It is good, Sajitteh. You stay here. After a few
sleeps the abomination will be caught. Your life can
start afresh."

"I've had two fresh starts already — my life being
upended to go to Nevéqilas — my planet being merged
with another planet by some bureaucratic error — I
don't want a third fresh start, Master Arbát."

"But what can you do?"

Sajit saw the despair in the old man's face. Arbát's
life, somehow, had become invested in Sajit's. But that
was not his problem. His problem was the chasm that
was opening up because his doppling was not there. "I
don't belong to you," he said. "And Tijas is *not* an
abomination."

"The Princeling must have given your family a
doppling kit, knowing this day would come. It was a
wrongful thing to do, against all nature, unless you
possessed the bloodline of Orifec —"

Which I do, Sajit thought. He wondered how much
Arbát really knew.

"Don't go, boy. Don't leave me. I'm old, can't you see that. I don't have much to live for these days." Arbát gripped Sajit's shoulders so tightly that he yelped. "No, no, I didn't mean to hurt you. I merely —"

"I have to find him."

"Don't you see, this is *why* doppling is such abomination. We are born to turn to others for love, for our deep needs. Not to an empty copy of our self. There's a reason for the prohibition. Look at you. A small child, obsessed within your self, unable to look out —"

"That's madness, Arbát. You can't ever know what it's like to be a doppling."

"But I need you!" the old man cried.

"Goodbye, Master, Thank you for all you taught me."

At this, Arbát began to weep, as though someone had died. Sajit had never seen the man so unable to control himself. There were dark issues in the man's obsession with his student, but Sajit knew that the love was real and that it ran deep.

"Don't think of us anymore, Arbát. It is *meúr.*"

"That which is unescapable is no less unbearable," said Arbát.

Sajit pitied Arbát, but the emptiness of Tijas's absence was more powerful than an old man's obsessions.

Sajit returned to his sleeping room and went back through the window toward the forest, taking nothing with him, not even a loaf.

***

Gharém returned to his ship without his equerry.

His time in the Temple of Aërat had enervated him, but the task ahead was swiftly bringing him back to life.

His ship, blackening a third of the sky even in the relentless daylight of Urna, had plunged much of Airang into winter. The park and the lake, in shadow, were bitterly cold; ice-flakes were forming, and the foliage was turning blue-red; dead loons floated.

Alone in his floater, ascending to dock with the belly of his great delphinoid, Gharém contemplated what was to come.

Only a few flocks of finding-birds had been released. Soon would come tens of thousands — soon they would black out what brightness remained in the sky.

Gharém slid past the irising airlock and entered an observation chamber in which all walls and floors had been deopaqued and were receiving images from outside; it seemed thus that he was standing on the air itself, looking at the world beneath, watching the crowd swarm in. The park itself had been cordoned off with forcewires.

Presently there came to him Kail Kruspar, the captain, and a dodecagon of childsoldiers that would serve as an honor-guard, four of them holding up sigils of Bellares, the military planet. The childsoldiers' eyes, like polished citrines, glowed soft, yellow, deadly light. They wore white tunics and belts of flame and stood on their hoverdisks, leaping, whirling, criss-crossing the air with streaks of eyelight.

And they cried out, in unison, the terrifying war-cry of the childsoldiers:

> *Ishá ha, ha, ha!*
> *Ishá ha ha hey ha!*

Lethal, the laser-lines arrowed the air, flinging up spiderwebs of death. No sound more elemental, more terrifying, more liberating than the prepubescent chorus of pure, focused destruction. Gharém loved the childsoldiers, children who burst into being like fireworks, who sizzled like the phosphorflies of Ont that live for but seconds, lived but to mate and die.

Gharém gazed down at the field below; they had cleared the park and in only a sleep or two they had built a pyramidal structure with a plateau on top, five-sided, and up each side a ramp with a slow-moving sliding stairway. The children would come to the ship from the world's five corners: lakeward, heartward, seaward, sunward, and nightward. Each side of the pyramid was painted in the colors of one of the five directions. In the park, children were already being herded in, processed, and allotted the stairway by which they would ascend to their destiny.

The five escalators, like silvery tentacles of a monstrous pentapus, met at the apex and the pyramid was crowned with a bulbous glazed pavilion; atop the pavilion a quincuncial arch was connected to a tubelike shaft that could suck the prospective childsoldiers, one by one, into the very belly of the delphinoid that hovered in the sky above.

"Ill take a floater down to the selection platform," he declared. No sooner had he sad this than the dodecagon of deadly children dissipated and reformed as two rows of five behind him, and two in front, holding aloft the inquestral sigils.

And together they shrieked, *Ishá há!*

Two servocorpse unrolled a displacement carpet and
Gharém and his honor guard stepped through —
        ***

"Tijas!" he shouted with his mind, knowing that to
shout with the voice could bring death. In the forest, he
tried to follow the echo in the back of his mind. But the
echo was faint. Tijas had done something to block him.
He was sure of it. But what? *Nothing can keep me out!*
he thought.

It grew dark.

And more dark.

So many times he had been in the forest alone. So
many times he had listened to the singing moons. So
many times he had sung to himself or chanted to the
strains of a crude whisperlyre.

Now he was alone but it was a different aloneness.

It was an aloneness that ached for the other half of
the self.   Not an aloneness that yearned for an
unknowable other, but an aloneness born of the
absence of an inalienable. Without Tijas, he was only
partly Sajit.

Sajit trudged through tall weeds, thorns scratching
through the worn clingfire of his tunic.

"Tijas!" his mind screamed again and again.

Then he tried shrieking out the name of his
doppling. *Crying out in the wildness, he heard no echo.*

Walking and weeping.   He went on.   Beyond
exhaustion. He must have been going in circles, for the
trees became first unfamiliar then familiar again. And
there was a kind of music in the air ... music that came

with the darkness ... music in the air itself. Music not made by nature, but in his mind.

The singing moons.

At last he came to the ruined temple, near where the displacement plate had taken them the time they had melded.

He spent the night in the roofless portico, under the moons. They sang, but their music gave no joy.

***

Veznávikas were blacking out the moons. Only Kalíth and Ralíth remained visible. The finding birds were swooping and wheeling. Each clutched a child in its claws.

Gharém stepped out onto the parapet atop the pyramidal quincunx.

Nineteen whisperlyres, one for each pillar of the High Compassion, began to sound, each played by a masked bard astride a pteratyger, arranged in ascending flights of seven, five, three, two, and two more that encircled each other like mismatched twins, one a giant, one a pup, the pattern called *denónikas*, the Nineteen Worlds.

The music twanged and reechoed as Gharém spread out his arms and legs in a cruciform pose, his head and limbs forming the Great Pentacle of Longing.

At his gesture the music was answered by nineteen cloud bugles, played by angelic servocorpses, their lips welded permanently to the srinjid mouthpieces of their instruments, who floated under the flocculent canopy of the sky, who represented the *denoshtálkas*, the nineteen starships that once came from the nineteen worlds to seed the Dispersal of Man.

Another motion of his hands and from the ground below came the stridulant harmonies of nineteen times nineteen automated shimmerviols. On the lake below came the boom of nineteen water-organs. From the treetops nineteen flocks of phantasmagoric pseudornithons.

The sky, the earth, the lake — chaos of unsynchronized sound — yet underlying it, a certain grim order. For chaos was Gharém's objective. From darkness and chaos came the High Inquest; from the Inquest came a kind of order, the fragile order that balances chaos with chaos. All other forms of order were heresy. That was why the childsoldiers existed — to nudge the human universe back to the perfect imperfection that was the High Compassion.

The children came from every world — collecting children was the only tax the High Inquest imposed on the twenty thousand worlds of the Dispersal. It was Gharém's supreme honour to serve the collection of this taxation. He had collected children of every hue — from the golden-skinned sylphs of Ákkathorn to the blue-hued angels of Ájumma.

Here on this backworld, the children were curiously nondescript — average in height, eye color, without extraordinary variances in skin tone — from a long isolation, perhaps, they had bred to a dull uniformity.

Armies were converging on the five escalators now, shoving, confused, babbling. From the parapet they seemed to swarm like insects, but when the reached the lowest rung of the escalator they were forced into single file.

Gharém sidled over to the nearest moving stair. There were hundreds of steps, and on each step stood a child.   Far below, their faces were a kaleidoscope of emotion: trepidation, anger, sorrow, unease, a few faces of fanatical courage or stoicism.

Did they cry for their mothers? But the journey up the escalator would soon transform these faces.   The stairs moved slowly and the constrained cacophony of many orchestras had a hypnotic effect; by the time they reached the parapet, each child seemed numbed, almost as it he had passed through a servocorpse factory and was now but a shell of a human.

"Welcome, my children," Gharém said.   They streamed toward him. But before they could reach him, they would reach the sucking tubes, and with a whoosh of air they were carried into the sky, into the five funnels which fed into a singe cone.   He could imagine the children, snapping from the trance of the music, flying around inside in a jumble.   This was the beginning of the process.   Disorient, confuse, erase the warmth of family, make them into empty vessels ready to receive the inerrant mastery of the High Compassion.

Since Man began it had always been children who had the fastest reflexes, the most pitiless instincts; for they grown into ambiguity.   They were the Inquest's naked will.

And all around they came to him from the five-fold stairway to the gateway to glory. Gharém shrieked with joy. Finding-birds wheeled and the music rose to engulf all other sounds.

***

The cry of the finding-bird is a rasp, metal screeching on unlubricated metal. It is a screech without any quailty of coming from a living creature. And now, as they threaded the deep night of the dancing moons, the screech came over and over. "Something's wrong," Mikkálu said. "The bird is flying in circles."

He and Éluma were watching. Orifec was not with them. The Son of the Starlight sat slumped against a far railing of the floater.

"Ori," she called to him. He did not look at her.

"Don't worry about him," Mikkálu said. "Things were better anyway. Before, when it was just you and me."

Éluma said, "He's hiding something. He knows something we don't know. I can tell."

Mikkálu did not know what it was. He tried to comfort her. She held him on her lap. Nuzzling against her chest, he found the curve of her breasts startling. "Not so innocent," she said softly. And kissed the top of his head.

"I'm still a kid," he said, "and you're not."

Time dilation had placed between them an unbridgeable gulf.

"But you still love me," she said. "As if it were yesterday."

"And you've seen so many things, staying pinned to a single spot in time, seen so much upheaval."

She held him.

"You're a childsoldier," she said. "You can slice me with a glance."

"Do you find that exciting?"   He laughed with bitterness beyond his years.

"It's all exciting to me," Éluma said, "because I am Love Itself.   Every incarnation of love — from the infernal depths to the most exalted."

"Can I kiss you?" he said.

"Anyone can," she said. "I am Aërat."

But before he could, the screeching came, louder and more grating. The bird was swooping, diving, flying in circles. Bucking between the moons. On the ground below, it careening skeins of reflected moonlight.

Orifec had come up to them now. He too was gazing at the bird as it darted and spun.   From its overhead movements came a

"The bird is crazy," Mikkálu said. "It's defective."

Éluma said, "Isn't its sole objective to zero in on someone's DNA?"

"There's no way it could be confused."

"But there is," Orifec said. "There is."

Fifteen

Planet of Dopplings

Sajit could not sleep. He felt *displaced*.
He was somewhere else.

He got up and paced in the portico, beneath the singing moons. But his mind was somewhere else.

Where would Tijas have gone?

Earlier, in the room, they had even been able to do a kind of merging with no displacement plate at all, just by thinking. But then there had been proximity. There had to be a clear system to how this could work ... not just an accidental interconnection of disparate selves.

Perhaps the displacement plate itself might yield a clue. In the moonlight he found his way there. It was a glint in the unkempt weeds. How to make it find Tijas? Somewhere in its memory, tied as it was to the planetary thinkhive, surely it had his coordinates.

Subvoking is a subtle thing, children learn it more slowly that audible speech. Until they learn it, they are tethered to their caretakers, for they cannot go far except by non-displacement means; a klomet is far to work, a hundred klomets in a floater is barely anywhere.

You must say something without saying it, yet still activate the vocal cords and the muscles of the throat and lips. You must articulate without a sound, yet as clearly as though the air had passed through your lungs and was being expelled from your lips. That is subvocalising. There were, from time to time, people unable to do it at all. They were doomed to lives of isolation. As children they sat in shadows, corners; as adults they were invisible.

Sajit felt like one of those people now. There was a language he did not know. Yet once, he had been able to access it. What was the key?

Tijas....

He reached out,   Over what distance could their

connection be felt? When they wandered the city, they had felt each other's pain, sometimes with terrifying immediacy, sometimes like an itch that couldn't be scratched; but inside the displacement they had not just felt what the other felt, they had *become* each other.

But what if one did not subvocalize with words, but with *song?*

Sajit carefully wiped away the weeds that obscured the center of the displacement plate.   Shards of the gleaming could be seen, reflecting the moons' light through gaps in the undergrowth. Sajit sat down, eased himself into the *savezhatá* position where his mind would be at its most open, most receptive to the underlying heartbeat of the cosmos.

Even person is like a musical tone, he thought. Each person has a certain pitch, a certain range of overtones. Even when people are similar, they still can be told apart, just as two notes can be only a *shrut* away from each other yet have each one a differing personality, a different color.

Tijas is trying to get away from me, Sajit thought. *But he can't stop thinking about me.*

Sajit settled into *savezhatá,* closed his eyes, thought of a tone, thought of *himself,* of the tone that most sounded like who he was.

He imagined himself a human whisperlyre, with all his cells like sympathetic strings, vibrating to the overtones of the fundamental tone. He imagined his own breath stirring the strings, one finger plucking a single note, letting it die away, squeezing it back to life, in the rhythm of his own heart.

A flash —

Tijas.

Running.

Let me find you!

There's nothing between you and me, Sajit thought. Not even a *shrut* within a *shrut.* We are the same string. We thrum together.

Tijas!

And suddenly, he was inside the great nothing....

***

Corridor.

Running.

No time to see the corridor, only to know it as a tube of pure force with walls of darkness. A corridor without end, and far far ahead a point of light, a flash that was Tijas.

You can't catch me!

Not true. The corridor accordioned shut with a shrill screech and now they were neck and neck and Sajit leaped into his doppling's shadow, and they were together again.

As they had lain together in the doppling kit, deep in amniosis.

The corridor telescoped open again.

"Where is this?" Sajit cried out.

It is everywhere. It is nowhere. He had answered himself.

The corridor closed in on itself. It twisted. It writhed, it coiled, it bent backward and always they were together, the still center of chaos.

***

"What do you mean," Mikkálu said, "there is? I've been with the Child Collector for sleeps of sleeps. These finding birds are not supposed to get confused. The only time I ever saw this —"

But Mikkálu didn't even want to think of it.

"It's something he has been hiding," said Éluma. "He's always been hiding it."

The *veznávik* flew in circles, its cries rending the air. Now it spoke in a metallic voice:

Glory to the High Compassion!

You are found, O child, lost, found, lost by the finding-bird!

But the bird had found nothing. It was going mad. It had encountered something it was not programmed for.

You are found! You are lost!

You are lost! You are found!

And the bird swooped and soared, chased its tail, screeched as the floater followed it, above the canopy of forest.

Mikkálu said to Éluma, "It could only happen if —"

The memory came to him, as disturbing as it had been then —

***

The planet was called *Karkárak*. It was a backworld, like Urna ... perhaps even more remote. There was only one inhabited landmass and it was dotted with spiky outcroppings, so that there was no area large enough to accommodate a formal Quincunx of Collection.

So the platform was built in the air, and droves of finding-birds sent out. It was Mikkálu's first outing as

Kyar Gharém's equerry.

It was a much leaner production than the spectacle in the park at Urna. Yet there was enough grandeur to stir any childsoldier's heart. First came five phalanxes of crack troops, shooting like a five-petaled firework into the sky, and as always the air resounding with the shrill cries of *Ishá ha!* Below them the surface was like the taut-stretched skin of an ankylosaur; on the spikes rested villages and tiny terraced farms; travel from village to village was effected by gliding between spikes on rickety boats hanging from strands of silky metal.

The music, too, was far more subdued than he would later be used to; there was only a mixed consort of shimmerviols and a pair of kalophonons bleating plaintively, and five nude servocorpses puffing away on iridium shofars.

But it was not the relative paucity of the music or even the weirdness of the spiny terrain that made the impression.

It was the finding-birds. Thousands upon thousands launched from the culling platforms, diving down towards the villages in the glow of two red setting suns; and suddenly —

All of them going insane! All of them flying in circles, crashing into each other, some dropping out of the sky into the crevices between the spikes of rock. And then, the ones that survived, descending with outstretched metal talons on the villages —

"What's happening, Kyar Gharém?" he blurted out, ignoring his duty which was to be utterly silent unless commanded to speak. Gharém was so startled he did not even slap the boy for his cheek — Mikkálu had already flinched instinctively.

"I don't know *everything*, you inquisitive monkey!" Gharém said.

Now the finding-birds were flocking together and reversing direction. They moved in orderly lines towards the platform. As they came closer Mikkálu saw the unthinkable; each *veznávik* clutched *two* children. And each pair of children looked identical.

It was nauseating. Each pair was even dressed alike, as if no attempt had been made to even conceal the horror that was doppling.

Mikkálu lost control. He ran to the edge of the floating pavilion and vomited over the railing. This was abomination! It was a violation of nature — *twins!* he could barely think the word. He clutched the railing and heaved.

And suddenly he felt Gharém's big hands on his shoulder. He felt a curious vibration and after a moment, he suddenly realized that the Child Collector was laughing.

"Inquisitive," said Gharém, "yet also ignorant."

"Thank you, my Lord," Mikkálu said, forgetting his customary cheekiness in his confusion.

"You come from a planet with the twin taboo," Gharém said. "You think twins are some kind of horrific aberration. Do you know that in some of the planets with this taboo, one is always killed at birth? So barbaric. Is yours like that?"

"My Lord, I've never even seen one. I just know that it's ... disgusting."

"For me, too, for a different reason. It messes up my quota. Come inside, boy, so you don't have to look at these 'abominations.'" Not unkindly, Gharém led the equerry into an inner room and deopaqued the walls. An astrogator, Kail Esmána, and an assistant worked over some thinkhives. A star map spread itself across the room. Gharém set the boy down on a chairfloat, and then sat down himself, across from him.

"Before I decide what to do," Gharém said, "I need to know why. Mikkálu-without-a-Clan!"

"Yes, my Lord."

"Awaken the planetary thinkhive."

Grateful to be given a job, Mikkálu subvocalized a command and an eidolon appeared. The thinkhive assumed the avatar of a wizened, simian creature with bluish fur.

"I am the High Inquest's lawfully ordained Collector of Children," Gharém said. "I command you to give me appropriate explanations. There seems to be an unusual number of twins here."

Mikkálu winced when he heard the word, and was amazed that Gharém could utter it without any kind of negative coloring.

The thinkhive laughed and said, in its clipped amd archaic thinkhive-like speech pattern, "High Inquest very very big! Our world very very far. Things happen here, not seen, not seen." A panorama of the world's history played out in holosculpt animation.

"A thousand thousand sleeps ago, plague. No help. Whole planet almost die. Compulsory twinning made law. Now whole culture change, everyone always paired, birth, sexual coupling, even death."

The thinkhive's eidolon popped out of being.

"What will you do, my Lord?"

"Stick to my mission," Gharém said. "What kind of backworld witchdoctory is this, with some kind of crude automatic doppling made compulsory? We have clear instructions from the High Inquest. One of each DNA imprint. Come, boy. Now you will see a vision of the awesome power of the High Inquest."

He grabbed the boy's hand and pulled him from the inner chamber. Once more they stood on the parapet. The air was thick with finding-birds, each with a child in each talon. Again Mikkálu's gorge rose, but now he tried to stifle it. This was a different culture. It had different taboos. Why, back in training in Bellares he'd met a boy on whose planet they routinely stoned to death men who loved other men. He remembered how horrified that boy had been when Mikkálu told him of an average day in the Temple of Aërat.

"I've got to stop being so provincial," he told himself. But the sight of so many twins was still unnerving.

Yet the next thing he saw was infinitely worse.

Gharém raised both hands, balled into fists, high above his head.   He closed his eyes, perhaps communicating with their own starship's central thinkhive. The birds became very still, hovering;

Gharém opened his left fist.

All at once each bird raised its left wing with a resounding *thwack* that made the very air snap and released its left talon.   A thousand children were released. A thousand children tumbled, to be impaled on the rocky spikes below. Mikkálu heard the collective scream, more like a howling wind than the sound of a thousand children. The scream followed by a wail from the survivors, a keening that pierced his soul, beyond sorrow.

"There," Gharém said.   "We were only ordered to bring back one of each."

"But you just killed a thousand people!"   Of course, one the rare occasions when twins were born, one was always killed.   But compassionately, and generally pre-partum. What kind of society would let abominations live, even base itself on them?

"I am sure they will be recycled by some servocorpse factory," Gharém said.   "Pretty little dead children are always in demand as servants."

And now the birds flew one by one onto the floating pavilion, each dropping its remaining child before folding itself back up into a compact silvery egg and rolling back into the storage area.

The platform was filling up with the Karkárak children.   They stood, bewildered, disoriented from the flight and from having seen their brothers and sisters tumble to their deaths.   Gharém's childsoldier attendants barked at them, moving them into lines, creating some semblance of military order.   Yet they broke ranks, huddled, whispered, clutched at one another, and always came the keening.

One *veznávik* remained.   It spread its wings wide, casting a ravenlike shadow over the crowd of children.

And spoke in ringing, optimistic tones:

Glory to the High Compassion!

These children have been preordained since birth to serve the High Inquest as childsoldiers, the most glorious of all occupations.   For childsoldiery is the straightest path toward receiving a clan-name and becoming more than an earthbound person.   It is the path to the stars.

Citizens of Karkárak, rejoice!

If your child survives, he will doubtless be someone of quality, someone with a true profession, someone whose clan will nurture and support for the rest of his life.

If your child falls, it is in the name of the High Compassion, which holds together the balance of the Dispersal of Man and on which all your lives depend.

Your children is a heroes!

All over the world, in village after village, these gilded words were raining from the sky ... along with the redundant children.

Mikkálu was looking up at the silvery bird with its outstretched wings blacking out the setting suns. He heard a thud behind him, then another.

Whipping round, he saw —

The new-minted childsoldiers were dropping, one by one, to the floor of the parapet. Crumpling up like dolls, falling down lifeless, each time hitting the pavement with the sound of a hollow skin drum.

"What's going on?" Gharém shrieked. "I forbid you to die!"

Mikkálu cried out, "My Lord, didn't you hear the thinkhive? It told us this would happen! *Everyone always paired, birth, sexual coupling, even death.* It told us they would die! They can't be apart!"

The kids kept toppling. Gharém did not even scold his equerry for impertinence, but seized his arm again and dragged him to the inner room. So furious was his demeanor that the pilot and the attendants scurried away. Gharém did not even remember to opaque the walls. As his master raged, Mikkálu saw the children's corpses pile up outside.

"My Lord —"

"You impertinent pipsqueak!" Gharém slapped the boy so hard that he reeled. And slapped him again, again, again, again —

"My Lord, I'm not a servocorpse," the equerry said, summoning up a shred of assertiveness.

Gharém stopped, looked at his hand, deep red from slapping the child. "Oh. I forgot," he said distractedly.

Then he added, "If you ever say a word about how I, Kyar Gharém, could not control myself, I shall have your laser-eyes gouged out."

"Of course not, Lord Gharém," Mikkálu said. "You know I keep all your secrets."

"Clean up my mess, then. Have the children placed in stasis; they are good, unblemished stock and will fetch a premium when recycled as servocorpses."

"Yes, Lord."

"And pick out a nice, voluptuous pleasure corpse from the cabinet, any gender. Make that one of each. And a phial of the finest dreamstuff. I need a thorough emotional draining before I report to the High Inquest. Remember, boy, I may beat you from time to time, but I too have a master."

It was the day that cemented the connection between Child Collector and equerry, the day Mikkálu found himself relieved of the routine of training on Bellares and found himself chosen more and more as this man's ... slave? jester? confidante? ... it was, in a way, a mutually vampiric relationship.

***

"Yes," Mikkálu said, "I *have* seen this before, once."

***

Get out of my mind! Tijas spoke without speaking. *Don't you know what will happen if we are both intertwined like this? I need you to get away from me.*

They tussled in the darkness.

— *But I can never get away from you.*

— *You must. Sajit, I was made for only one thing, and now the time has come and I have to do what I was made for. I was made to live an alternate life for you, to die an alternate death.*

— *No* —

Both materialized on a displacement plate in the middle of an open field. It was dawn.

"I told you not to follow!" Tijas said.

In that moment the shadow of the finding-bird fell across them. The air was all talons now. They were caught up. There was a rush of wind, thundering in their ears. Each was grasped firmly in a claw of the finding-bird. The boys reached out, clasped hands.

Together, they both said with their minds, *no matter what.*

The bird flew straight at the rising sun. And presently Sajit heard a sound above the wind.

It was a woman, screaming in terror.

A woman screaming as if she had seen some nameless nightmare, some unimaginable horror.

It was his mother.

Sixteen

I am not a Thing

Suddenly, the bird was descending, landing, and Orifec saw that the thing he most dreaded had happened. The find-bird had plucked both children away.

Éluma was screaming. The revulsion felt by an Urna native on seeing the order of nature negated — Orifec understood it, even though he himself was a doppling. She had not been prepared for this. He blamed himself.

And the two boys stood, their hair ragged from the whipping of the wind, two shadow-slim lads with the eyes of Aërat, who is Love personified.

"Mother —" they both said.

"How? How? One of you isn't mine. One of you is a demon, a thing of the dark."

And Mikkálu said, "I knew it. And so did you, Starry Highness."

"How can I tell which one is my true son?" Éluma cried.

Orifec answered, "They are both as true your sons as each other. Both were born from our love, even though one of them was nourished in an artificial womb."

"How can you stand there and tell me this?"

One of the boys spoke. "I am Tijas," he said. "I was birthed from a doppling kit. Sajit and I are one flesh."

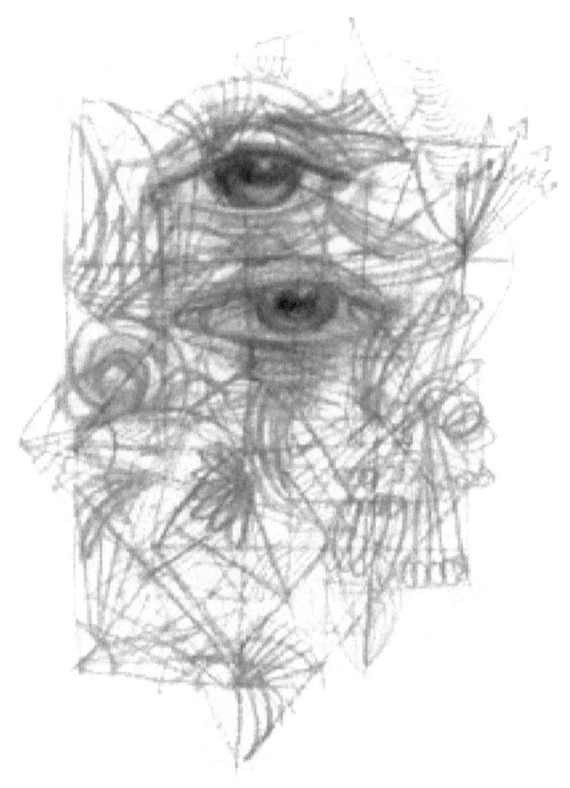

Orifec said to Éluma, "How can you cry abomination over some one we made together? You know very well that *I* am a doppling."

"That's different. You're a Princeling. A God, really. You renew yourself eternally, passing your memories on through the generations. That's not for mortals. It's blasphemy."

"But you yourself are a goddess, Éllekeh." Orifec reached out but she flinched.

"Get rid of it," she said.

Tijas said, "That's all I ever wanted, mother." She shuddered; Orifec was moved. "When the palace sent the doppling kit to the village, it was so that when the Child Collector came, I would be the one to go, to fight, to die in a blaze of glory, and Sajit would remain, grow into the greatest bard in the Dispersal. My death is part of the plan."

"No!" Sajit cried out. "You are part of me as no one else can ever be. I won't let you —"

"— lift the shadow from your life," Tijas said, and Orifec saw that Éluma marveled, how they finished each other's sentences. "I was *born* for this, brother —"

"You weren't *born* at all. You sprang full grown from the box because I awakened you —"

"— when you shouldn't have. When the Inquest came calling, that was the time to quicken me and hand me over and forget that there was once a mysterious box lying around in your breakfast circle."

"But I *had* to quicken you. Or I would never have been complete."

"I've heard enough," said their mother. "You break down the boundaries between person and person. Your existence is a blight on nature —"

Then Mikkálu said, "No, no, Ellekeh. I've been to other worlds. I've seen places where twins are not *haram*. I was on a world where there were *only* twins. The first time I saw them, I vomited. I know better now."

"Are you mad, Mikkeh?" Éluma said.   "I am Love Herself. I am all the values of this world. I can't accept this."

But Orifec saw the boys and knew that he loved them both.   They stood, frightened, close to each other, as the floater drifted — aimlessly for the moment — the morning sun glistening in their windswept hair.   And the eyes. Éluma's eyes. The love he felt was beyond logic, beyond rhetoric. He knew that he could not take back this love.

"I sent the doppling kit ... as protection, Sajit.   I didn't think ... there was *another* Sajit inside it. Another you. Another son whom I must love.   I've seen you together so many times ... I cannot say one is real and one is false ... I was the only one who knew ... and I understand you. I understand the loneliness of being cut off from myself. For I too am a doppling."

But Éluma was unmoved.   Her face was anger and revulsion. Orifec could not answer her. He knew he should have told her, knew also that telling would not have helped.   The laws of culture were far more unyielding than the laws of nature.

And the one who said he was Tijas cowered, unable to meet Éluma's gaze.

He said softly, "I'll go to the collecting place, Starry Highness."

"No," said Orifec.

"Yes, father," Tijas said. "This is what you made me for. You always knew that Sajit might be Collected. You broke the sacred law. You had the doppling kit sent to the house of Areon Dar-Sajit. You caused Arbát to be our tutor.   You had us brought to the citadel of

Nevéqilas. This is the destiny you made for me, Starry Highness. You are a Princeling. If you made me for a reason, who am I to go against your plan?"

The finding-bird flapped its wings.

"I don't care about any plan," Sajit cried. "Tijas is my brother, more than my brother, he's me! The plan went haywire the moment I activated the doppling kit."

"And because you are my brother, more than my brother, because you're *me,* because I only exist for you," Tijas said, "I will become what I was made to become."

Orifec said, "No, no. Do you remember when I first knew there were two of you? Do you remember when I called you from your hiding place? What did you say to me, Sajit?"

"I said, *His* name *is Tijas.*"

Orifec said, "That is where you broke the natural order, Sajitteh. You gave him a name. Do you know how doppling kits were first invented?"

"No, father," Sajit said.

Orifec saw that Éluma was still half collapsed in rage and revulsion. How could he help her understand, when the sight of twins was a trigger for people of this world, evoking millennia of ingrained hatred? "Éluma," she said gently, "I'm telling you, as one who has learned a lot about other worlds, that your terror of dopplings is as illogical as any other taboo. In the ancient world, twins were feared as monstrosities. As were those who were left-handed, or palely pigmented, or who enjoyed sexual congress with unacceptable partners, or enjoyed the fruit of some tree or another. Urna's taboo is as illogical as any of these.

"But doppling kits were invented in a world where people did not fill their brains with consciousness. Their contents were simply sources of replacement organs, no more sentient than the kits themselves. Yet there were those who wanted a copy of themselves, a living copy they could love, who would understand them. Thus the technology came to be abused in some worlds."

"Ori, this is abomination. I don't care what learned explanation there is for it. The phantom child must die! It *must!*"

"But Sajit *named* him."

"Father is right," Sajit said. "Things do not have names. Tijas is not a thing."

"No, I'm not," Tijas said. "And because I am a person, I choose this for myself. I choose to die for my brother, my friend, my lover, my other self."

Orifec watched as Tijas embraced his brother. They kissed. Neither as lovers, nor as brothers, but as something other; something to be envied, not loathed. They were beautiful as a song is beautiful. He had an overpowering urge to protect them.

"Revolting!" Éluma cried. "This wounds me. I am Love. Love can't be mocked. Mikkálu — *kill the doppling.*"

Tijas turned his back on them all. He called out to the finding-bird, the ritual formula of submission to the High Inquest: *"Jātái evéndek hokhkeliassá* — May I live forever in the High Compassion."

The bird spread its wings wide, perched by the rim of the floater, poised to envelop the boy, claws, wings, and all.

"Mikkálu, laser him!" Éluma cried out "If you love me, kill him!"

"If you love me, Éluma," Orifec said, "don't say that."

The bird's claws stretched out like a stepladder. Tijas approached, was about to step, and the wings were about to enfold him —

Orifec saw that Sajit, too, was walking resolutely toward the *veznávik*. He could not bear it. He ran to shield them and —

— Leaped up throw his arms around his sons and — *"Laser him!"*

Mikkálu swooped up on his hover disk, spun, his eyes dilated and turned bright yellow —

Orifec felt blinding pain. He blacked out.

***

Sajit fell to the floor of the floater and the finding bird, gripping Tijas tight, soared skyward, wheeled overhead.

The slice of laser eyes cauterizes as well as cutting clean through flesh. Sajit saw half-Orifec, just above the thighs, and the other half lying inert. The upper half of his father was still alive. Sajit knelt beside him. The pain must be unbearable. Éluma knelt too. They did not meet each other's gaze.

Mikkálu whispered, "I'm sorry."

Sajit and his mother glared at each other. He had known her most as a woman cloaked in shadow. Could this woman really have given him life, was it this that gave her the right to his life away? Now, Sajit realized, he knew her not at all.

Mikkálu kept talking, talking too fast, trying to fill

in the awful silence. "I didn't mean to kill him. I didn't mean to kill anyone. You said *if you love me* — Éluma, you know I've always loved you, I'd cross the universe for you —"

"Be quiet, Mikkeh. I know you didn't mean this," Élumeh said. "But now he's dying. Orifec, our Starry Highness, is dying. And he has no successor."

"*You* killed him, mother," Sajit said, pitiless. "This man loved me. He gave everything to protect me. He's always known about Tijas, and he loved both of us. You can't understand. You'll say you love me, too, but you tried to kill me. Tijas *is* me. We're more than biological twins, we're dopplings."

"I'm not dead yet," Orifec gasped. "Sajitteh ... summon the thinkhive of my palace."

"How?" Sajit said. "We're not even *in* the palace."

But they were; the floating parapet was still an extension of Orifec's domain ... but Orifec was weakening fast. There was no blood, only the smell of burnt flesh and a pair of dead legs severed just above the thighs. Sajit subvoked and the palace's regenerative mechanisms began to activate. Fleshy tendrils snaked up from the floor and attached themselves to the princeling. A fine mesh of flesh simulant wrapped itself around the wound. Injectors pumped analgesics and and poured a fuming mélange of anti-devivement reagents over his face.

"You won't die, Starry Highness," Sajit pleaded. "Tell me you won't die." For Orifec seemed revived.

"I will, my son," Orifec said. "Your doppling will take your place among the childsoldiers. And you will rule Urna as its first true artist-prince."

"I won't become you," Sajit said softly.

"I daresay not," Orifec said. "I became all my other selves. But ... you needn't."

Sajit cried, "What Urna anyway? Urna will soon be completely sucked into Alykh. Even if I *could* be a Princeling, I'd be Princeling of a room in a ruin."

Why was he even speaking to them? He could feel Tijas being carried on the wind. He could feel Tijas' terror. And the love that had made him willing to throw away his very identity.

"Mikkálu!" Sajit said. "Where is the finding-bird going?"

"To the collecting grounds, Sajit. In the old days, it was a park by the Lake of Luminous Loons."

"Do you know how to fly this thing?"

"No, but ... I think you can."

"Yes ..." Orifec said faintly. "You subvoked and got the regenerators to activate. Years ago ... I keyed the palace thinkhives with your bio-signature. I wanted you to have ... all this." Orifec actually smiled. "Ironic, no? But I want to see a little more ... I'll ... cling to life a while."

"Not a while," Sajit said. "We'll get you plugged into a proper iatromaton when we get back. And I'm going to go and save Tijas."

The goddess of love wailed ... it was the cry of a dying loon ... the death-screech of a deactivating thinkhive. Mikkálu stared at her, at Sajit, at the half-man he had created.

"I'm sorry, I'm sorry," he kept repeating. "I never ever did that before ... I never misused my killing gaze. I was confused ... because ... how much I love Éluma."

Sajit wanted to pummel him with his fists. But the boy had laser eyes.

"Poor Mikkeh," Orifec said, growing fainter. "You don't even know what love is."

Sajit squeezed his father's hand. "I can't forgive him," he said. "And I'll *never* forgive *her*."

Éluma said softly, "My son, my son." She had ceased her keening and now sat whimpering.

"I *had* mother," Sajit said. "She perished when the people bins came. I had a father too, and siblings. They're all gone down and now there's only you and a dying father and my other self ripped out of me. My life has been chopped in two."

It all came flooding back. Attembris. Circles of starlight. A life without a doppling, without a goddess for a mother and a princeling for a father. Chanika, Vimla ... why had he not thought of them since all this happened? So many feelings, so many images — guilt. Grief. Self-hatred.

Éluma stood up now. She spoke tonelessly, beyond emotion. "Urna is undone," she said. "The laws of nature aren't working anymore. *Things* are people. Abominations are my children. I've given the man I love a death-blow."

"No, Ellekeh," Mikkálu said. "The world is a different world. We have to change."

"I can't change," Éluma. "I am eternal. I am the Unchangeable Truth of Urna. I am Love."

And with great deliberation she walked to the edge of the parapet, and leaped.

***

Mikkálu ran to the railing. He saw her fall. She did not flail. She had a sereneness to her. Her garment flapped about and hid her face.

"Ellekeh!" he cried out and began to weep, not caring that the flooding tears could warp the alignment of his laser-irises. A random spark flew from his left eye, slicing an upper railing. The wind whistled.

He had to save her. He summoned his hoverdisk and hopped on, sending it spinning, adjusting its trajectory with quick subvocalizings so the disk would swoop down fast enough to catch up with gravity. Wind whipped his face and dried his tears.

She plummeted. He sped. They were above a forest. He overtook her, swept upward, seized her by an arm. "Let go!" she screamed, the wind drowning her out.

Mikkálu took control. His training made it easy. He folded an arm around her waist, held her face up. Instinctively, she clung to him — though she may have wanted to die, her body couldn't help holding on —

He braked hard. The wind slapped at them. Mikkálu headed for a treetop — a maneuver he'd done many times in battle, to gain the high ground.

He decelerated quickly, tried to find the softest spot in the thicket. It was a cottonsilk tree; balancing himself on a branch and clutching Éluma's waist, he bored some criss-cross scratches in the bark with his eyes, and a misty white sap came spewing out, solidifying as it hit the air and weaving itself into a cushiony, bed-like mass.

Mikkálu moved Éluma into the densest part of the sap; it wove itself around her, keeping her from falling.

"You can't fall anymore," he told her, "not until I cut

you free."

"I won't go back to Orifec."

"No. They are long gone. I'm sure they didn't wait around to see if you'd survive the fall. And I'm sure they are not waiting for *me*. They must hate me."

"Mikkeh, don't do this! I *have* to die! It's the only right thing to do."

"Calm down. I'll take you to the temple."

"Temple?" she cried. "You know I can't go there anymore. I've birthed an abomination. I'll never be clean again."

Mikkálu said, "I am still a child, Éllekeh, but I have loved you all my life. Soon I'll be too old to be a childsoldier. When I reach puberty I'll lose these lightning reflexes. I'll grow awkward. But then I'll be old enough. And I'll come for you."

Éluma even managed to smile. "I'll be an old woman on your next trip. Time dilation is the killer."

"If we're doomed never to be the perfect age for each other," he said, "I don't care. You are Love."

"Don't you understand? I *was* Love. Now I'm no one. Love is dead on our world now."

"If you're not a goddess, what are you?"

"A whore," she said.

And she kissed him, a comfortless, cold kiss.

Yet he still loved her for it.

***

Sajit said, "Now there's only you and me."

"Don't be angry at your mother," Orifec said. "She's panicking because she's lost her anchor — her whole belief system. And she's a goddess, a guardian of that system."

"I'll try not to hate her. Or Mikkálu. He was torn, too."

"Where will we go now?" Orifec said. Sajit could see that he was visibly weakening. Orifec's breathing was irregular. The regenerators were only of moderate strength, cut off from the main thinkhives of the palace and without access to the rarest of medications.

"We'll go to the palace. We will save your life."

"But that's not what you're thinking, Sajitteh. You want to go to the Lake of Luminous Loons. You want to save your brother."

"Can he be saved?"

"I don't know," Orifec said. "You have gone far beyond the rulebook already."

"Can *you* be saved, father?"

"I also don't know. Perhaps. The life is draining from me. I'm not in pain. Enough analgesics are being pumped into me to numb an army. But it means that when I die, I will just turn off. Like an opaquing wall."

"What will I *do?*"

Orifec said, "You'll do what your heart tells you. And I will agree with you, because, Sajitteh, I *made* your heart."

The floater flew northwards, toward Nevéqilas. They did not speak for a long time.

Sajit knew where he must go. His heart had spoken. And he that Orifec, too knew.

So in silence they flew, as night began to fall. One by one, the moons rose.

Eríkion danced in the lowering sky. Kalíth and Ralíth began their stately figure-eight.

Half-Harikozmá hung low, misshapen, blue-green.

Slowly, the stars were coming out.

Here, in the emotional extremity between the inconsolable and the unattainable, between grief and revelation, between love and disillusion, he heard something he had never heard in any other place but the clearing in the woods in Attembris.

He heard the moons singing.

Seventeen
Ina and Areon

On the day the sky fell, Areon and Ina and the daughters had been in their apartments, and the day had gone normally at first.

Until they had told Sajit the truth about the box. And about his parents.

Then Sajit left. They had not thought anything of it. Sajit often wandered off. He was an independent spirit, Ina reflected, and now that he realized he was not even related to them ...

The boy had never belonged to them.

Ina had tried. There was something — aloofness, perhaps — or *otheworldliness* — he often did not even seem to be present.

When he hugged her, he would seem even more remote, as though slipping right through her.

Ina had tried to be a mother to him. Eventually she did not try that hard.

It was almost a relief to tell him the truth, though she did not want to admit it to herself.

When he walked away, of course, she assumed he would be back after one his moody walks.

And then people started raining from the sky.

***

Their apartment was in the shadow of the crystal stem of Nevéqilas. Their rooms had no physical windows — they were not *that* highly placed in the hierarchy — but all the walls could change to afford views over many parts of the city. And the girls had been watching the Lake of Luminous Loons —

Criss-crossing the lake in zebra lines of light —

And their cries, carried electromagnetically across the city, close as though they were positioned at the lake's edge —

Vimla looked up and the vista followed her gaze. And she cried out, "Mother, mother, its raining people!"

Quickly Ina deopaqued all the walls all around so they could see what was happening. They were really falling out of the sky. Like a shower of dark meteors. People in stasis, in every possible position, curled up, stretched out, scrunched, unfurled, frozen in a moment that could have been a century or more ago. And above them, people bins, disgorging their contents. People were pelting down like multicolored hail.

Ina had heard of these things. She never expected it to happen here. People bins were always emptied out on empty worlds. This was a mistake.

And the High Inquest *never* made mistakes.

She said to Vimla — Chanika was huddled in a corner, whimpering — "Sit tight. We're trapped ... all we can do is watch."

Then she heard — distant but persistent — a shrill, terrifying chorus —

> *Ishá há! Ishá há!*
> *Ishá ha ha héy ha!*

and knew it was the sound of childsoldiers. So faint yet so relentless. And it was getting louder.

She subvoked a quick command to the windows and the view changed to just outside Nevéqilas. That's when she saw they were coming.

It was a swarm. They were like bees, like birds, but in a precise formation, the space between them exactly the same. On their hoverdisks, they spun, cartwheeled, figure-eighted in tight formations.

The chant grew louder —

The images on the walls began to fracture —

The walls split open —

And then the earth shook, and their home fell on top of them.

***

They could not perform their children's death ceremonies. They had not even been able to retrieve their bodies. Ina and Areon had survived the initial wave by a miracle — two walls collapsing inward to form a tent that led to an opening and a corridor and a balcony that swung precariously, attached to the crystal stamen by a few metallic strands.

Areon had succumbed a day later, in the street, with no way to treat his injuries. Servcorposes took him away, perhaps to a factory where the body could be refurbished and made of use to someone, though Ina did not know what services remained in the broken city of Shirensang.

Servocorpses had cleared some rubble and Ina found that she had a little cave that had once been a spacious apartment. The doppling kit and a few random decorations remained. She sat, in a corner. One of the walls, a jagged fragment could still project some images of the outside world. She subvoked a few commands and she could see the metal spiders throwing up an alien city.

She sat by herself most days, eating little — in what was left of the plaza outside, they were distributing what they called the *Princeling's Bounty*, though no one had seen the ruler of Urna at all. The bounty was sometimes a bunch of *gruyesh*, sometimes a parcel of flatcakes or a jar of darkberry jam. They came from the royal stores, so there was still some kind of system in place, a government, even. She saw no one.

She was unable to grieve ... it had all been so sudden, and now it was all locked away in some other world, a world that had had some order to it.

Once she found her way to the Temple of Aërat. She saw supplicants coming and going, but they looked alien — they even smelled alien. And they acted not like worshippers, but more like clients.

Sajit could not be located.

Perhaps he was dead.

But ... what if he wasn't? Could she even find him?

She thought of crossing over to the new city ... but no, surely, that was too alien, too disturbing to think of. And so she drifted in and out of the ruined apartment, eating little, just waiting for something ... waiting to join the rest of her family ... waiting for some kind of ending.

***

And then, a childsoldier appeared at the door. He was slim. He carried his hoverdisk slung around his waist. His skin was an unusual brown she had not seen in the city, his cheeks bore tattoos of firephoenixes that seemed to flap their wings. His expression was pitiless, but he spoke gently.

"Greetings, mother," he said. "I am Tarash-without-a-Clan and I am tasked by the Inquestral Child Collector to find a boy named Sajit-wthout-a-Clan, patronymic Dar-Areon. Is he here?"

"Your friends killed all my children," she said bitterly, "and we don't even know why."

"Not Sajit," the boy said, his eyes gleaming citrine. "Our thinkhives don't show any erasure of his DNA signature."

Something stirred in Ina's deadened soul. Sajit was not dead.

"Don't be worried, Ina Des-Areon. Yours will be a glorious motherhood," said Tarash. "If Sajit lives he will receive a clan-name and become one of those who travel freely between worlds, with a true vocation and a meaningful future. You will be proud. And if does not live, he will become one with the High Compassion."

"You're telling me he isn't dead.   You're telling me that even though he's alive, you're planning to take him away and ... almost certainly ... kill him."

"Death is but a doorway to the High Compassion, blessed mother Ina," he said, giving her the title properly due to a mother of one who might become a martyr in the name of the High Inquest. "I'll come calling again," he said.   "Or else, my commander will release a finding-bird.   Wherever he may be, it'll manage to bring him to us.   My commander is Lord Gharém, whose collection rate is known to be perfect."

"If you find him, where will you take him?"

"To the Lake, where we have built our collecting station.   Your son will ascend the quincuncial escalator and be pulled into the belly of a great warship.   And then he will ride the overcosm to Bellares, the warrior world.   If you would care to see him, to say goodbye to him ... you could try waiting there.   He'll come, eventually."

***

When the boy had gone, she tried to open the doppling-kit, even knowing that an abomination lay inside it.   Surely to see a not-Sajit in the box would make her go mad.

Yet if a monster lurked inside it, that monster could go off to Bellares and die and her son would still be alive, somewhere in this world.   He could still be found.

But nothing she could do would force it open, and when she pounded her fists against it, it rang hollow. Perhaps it had been a hoax from the beginning.

***

And so it was that she found herself in the park. The five-sided pyramid had sprung up right in the center, with the lake to one side, the woods to the other, and in the distance an alien city, thrumming and flashing and pounding as new buildings were being put up, new edifices arriving in a blink or two, the skyline clattering as new pre-formed city pieces were bolted into face by spiderlike robots.

And behind them the ruins. Urna was still a world, but it was a world rapidly being subsumed. It had already, in fact, ceased to be; what was happening now was just a bit of cleanup.

In the park were children and their relatives. Weeping, saying goodbye, exchanging last embraces. Five cordoned pathways led to the five escalators. Childsoldiers held back the throng, clearing the pathways. Ethereal music played from the sky, the water, the trees. Above was the delphinoid warship, blotting out many of the moons. It was the circling loons that lit the park, and the soft werelight suffusing the musical ensembles that played from every direction.

Ina made her way aimlessly at first. Seeing all the goodbyes made her feel even emptier; she had not been able to say goodbye to anyone.

Taking advantage of the crowd, food vendors had set up portable stalls. There was even an open air theater with dancing servocorpses and a magician pulling hats out of lizards.

The festival atmosphere blended incongruously with the general grief. But as she pushed her way through to the barricade, the sense of loss was more powerful, radiating from everyone as they pressed against the barrier built from cones of glittering metal linked with strands of force.

The forceropes were invisible but strong. You could feel your way to the gaps, slide your arms through a little way. Many of the families were doing that. Little siblings, grandparents, all trying to touch their children for the last time. For even if they lived, there was time dilation; a year could pass in the life of the soldiers, and this past would already be unreachable. It was goodbye beyond the parsecs that would soon separate them.

Children filed past, solemn, staring straight ahead, transfixed by their own role in the spectacle.

She did not see Sajit.

A hand brushed her shoulder and softly whispered her name.

Shocked, she turned. "Master Arbát!"

***

He had been coming to the collecting field for many days now, with some vague notion of snatching Sajit away ... Sajit or Tijas. Or both. Arbát had no clear idea of what he would do, what he *could* do. But he was drawn to the collecting field.

"You think he's alive, too, don't you?" said Ina Des-Areon.

Arbát did not answer. He was trying to figure out how much she should know.

"You've *seen* him," Ina said.

Arbát said, "I have."

At that moment, there came a raucous blast from the five-sided pyramid. The elevators reversed; children began to descend.   From the platform there came five iridium shofars, each held aloft by three servocorpses, and they blared a terrifying music above which sounded a thunderous voice:

"The collection will now pause for one sleep and resume after a revolution of your world, so that the collected may be processed and stored and room made for the as-yet-uncollected.

"Rejoice, O men and women who are subjects of the High Compassion!   Listed children will be found and trained to serve the High Inquest.   Every listed child will be collected.   Do not hide your children, do not shield them from their glorious future.   Find them, bring them, say your farewells."

And then, bursting from the heavens, came the high-pitched massed voices of a million childsoldiers, singing the Inquestral anthem:

Dhelyá sarang z tóraka z nishis
hokhtin verapo pa' jitaaren mi
pa' zérveras, pan qériah dídeas mi...

I, a slave, a chattel, a nothing
throw before you all my heart
my thoughts, the works of my hands....

It was transcendent, overwhelming: the fervent, full-throated keening of a million young voices — utterly beautiful, utterly pitiless — the awesome, unchallengeable power of the High Inquest that had held the balance of the cosmos for twenty millennia. A sound of consummate beauty and terror.

The anthem rang out and many dropped down in genuflection.   Some sobbed.   The song reached its climax with the words

Eih auraín aiunaín
min yverprendéis práxein
suvitek, chom nikans ebrenden

Yrshíltraor — Urázbedar —
Eih eih hohk'kelassiaísti mun
dheyáin z tóraken z níshien

At the final hour
you will take me up into your arms
suddenly, as in a planet's destruction

Protector — Skyfather —
bless me with the High Compassion
I, a slave, a chattel, a nothing.

And all at once fell darkness; with a single movement the entire army had turned and displaced itself onto the ship, for each hoverdisk contained a homing displacement plate.

And the sky blackened with a single thunderclap.

"We have some time," Arbát whispered.   We need not watch here.

"Come, Master Arbát," Ina said.   "I've had no one to talk to for so long. Tell me how you came to see my son. Tell me how you know he is alive."

"I'll tell you everything," Arbát said, though that was not his intention. There was, however, a reason to cultivate Sajit's mother. The reason had been forming in his mind ever since the boys fled from Attembris. It was the reason he had come to the collecting field, after looking in vain for Sajit's family amid the disintegrating palace of Nevéqilas.

Gingerly, he took her hand — she clutched it, making him nervous, for no one had clung to him in this way for many decades — and they threaded their way through the crowd; a few displacement plates still worked and they could back to the ruined palace in a few jumps, with a detour or two.

When he saw how she was living he wondered how she had survived at all. The family's generously appointed rooms had been reduced to half a chamber, half filled with rubble. But when Arbát saw what he had been looking for, it was hard for him to contain his excitement.

The memory of his ecstatic, pained relationship with his two pupils who were one came flooding back — the shameful moments as much as the joyful ones — the moments when he knew he nurtured a talent far greater than his own, the moments when he wanted to be more than a teacher and tried to assuage his desire with servocorpses and fantasy ... all of it came back when he saw the box lying in the corner.

"Is that —" he asked her.

"If only I had never seen the cursed thing!" Ina said. "But it can't save us now. I can't even get it open. And it's very light. It's empty. Somehow it must have aborted — as it should have — I should never have accepted to spawn an abomination in my home."

Arbát told her that his own rooms were less

damaged — in fact practically intact, though he embroidered a little; the amount of living space remaining to him was as small as this, but he had not started off with a residence for a family of five and servocorpses and under the special favor of the Starry Highness. "Perhaps I could store a few of your things," he added.

Thus it was that not by lying, but more by omission, Arbát came to be in possession of the doppling kit.

... to be continued

with Jaroslav Olša, well known Czech science fiction personality and diplomat, at the launch of the first Czech edition of Somtow's stories in 2019, in Prague

Interview by Tomaš Bazika

An interview with Thai-American composer-conductor Somtow Sucharitkul about his most recent opera and his work on Paul Spurrier's film *Eullenia*

I. Helena Citrónová:

The real character of your new opera Helena Citrónová is not free from controversy. A Jewish concentration camp inmate who had a love affair with a German camp guard. What drew you to this subject?

I discovered the story of this opera in a BBC documentary about Auschwitz. There was an interview with Helena and the story was very haunting. It was not a story about a triumphant love. It was full of ambiguity. It makes you ask all sorts of questions about the nature of love itself. I try to avoid answering any of the questions in the opera. I just want to present the story almost exactly as it happened according to the documented historical record. In a very real sense, the story came to represent to me what the holocaust really meant. Because it was not about people being horrible to other people. Of course, that happened. What it was really about was one group of people telling another group of people that they are not human. And in doing so, destroying their own humanity. Because the more you take away the humanity of other people, the more you reduce your own humanity. To me Helena was a great hero because she refused to give up who she was.

How is it relevant today – why should people care?

It's relevant today because people have not learned their lesson. Many ears ago, I started working with the Israeli, German and Czech embassies in Thailand about teaching young people about the Holocaust. I asked me students whether Thailand lost or won in the Second World War and they didn't know the answer. Somebody had to tell them. This was when I started working on this, creating different programs each year. In a sense, producing this opera on the 75th anniversary of the liberation of Auschwitz is basically a culmination of all these other works that I have done. It's not just to teach local children about it. It's about reminding everybody that the Holocaust is about six million people and it's also about six million individuals.

What role does Helena's moral ambiguity have in your opera?

If you look at the story completely dispassionately, you might accuse the two people of having a selfish and transactional sort of relationship. That is one possible way of looking at the facts. It's in contrast to this "great passion that conquers the universe" theme, which is another way of looking at it. Perhaps both of those stories are present. In the end it is a story about redemption. Therefore I don't buy the sordid, transactional interpretation. In the opera you will see that the other girls call her a whore.

Is your own view of the real-life Helena reflected in the opera?

I wouldn't have written an opera about her if I didn't see her as an extremely inspired character, despite some elements of ambiguity. I feel she represents for me a complete refusal to allow somebody to take away one's personhood, no matter how awful the circumstances were. I think that Franz Wunsch even said afterwards that this is the lesson she had taught him. He felt somehow redeemed. Of course he may have been making it up for the judges. Who knows? But there is a deep truth in the story that we can all learn from. There was some fear on the part of some Israelis when they heard that I was writing this opera that by making it a love story between "the bad guys" and the victims that somehow they were being made sort of equal. If you read the libretto or look at the opera that's completely untrue. There is absolutely no whitewashing of the evil. The first time you see the hero of the story he shoots an old man in the head and Helena sees this. That's an incident that I created – it's not in the historical record – because I wanted the audience to realize right away that this is not a misunderstood Nazi little boy. I wanted people to realize he was part of this operation.

What is the lesson you would like the audience to consider?

I think it's most important for people to see themselves in this work. To not think of it as some remote history in a fantasy universe that could never happen again. Things like this have happened again already. And it's because we didn't learn the lessons enough.

You premiered an orchestral suite from Helena in Slovakia and in the Czech Republic this September. How was it received?

Well, I was quite frightened because, you know, Slovakia is Helena's country. I had no idea how people would react to some total stranger bursting in on somebody else's history. It was heartwarming because the reception in the places that were most involved in the story was extremely positive and enthusiastic. And it was then that I understood that the opera seems to have something to say to everyone. One of the most exciting things that happened was that the Slovaks immediately started the discussion about opening the opera in the National Theatre in Bratislava. This is already in talks. I was very happy about that. It was kind of a validation of the idea of universality in the story. I am having similar questions in Thailand. Why in the hell are you doing this? This has nothing to do with you. I mean, in a sense, not to say something is kind of complicity.

What are your expectations for the premiere of Helena in January 2020?

Well, the Bangkok premiere is happening in January and this production will go to Europe. I don't know. I'm actually quite frightened [laughs] because we are opening this opera in a country where there's a fast food chain called Hitler Fried Chicken and where a common slang in Thai for stingy is "Jew". This is amazing because as far as I know the actual number of Jewish people that the Thais may have met in person is probably almost non-existent. For some reason, many of the tropes of this have infiltrated this culture. We had to do a lot of explanation about why Hitler Fried Chicken is not cool.

II. *Eullenia:*

You made a new recording – the first recording in Thailand – of Carlo Gesualdo's music for Paul Spurrier's film *Eullenia*. Do you recall your first conversation with Spurrier about your involvement in the film?

He consulted me about it. He said that the character of the crazy composer Gesualdo is deeply rooted in the story. The fact that there is a serial killer who sort of bases himself on Gesualdo means that you can't just have a random piece of music. It had to be that [Gesualdo's] piece of music. And then he looked around for a version that he could buy the rights to. I pointed out I always wanted to do a lot of Gesualdo here and that this should be a good excuse for me to do an all-Gesualdo concert. Or maybe doing the concert was a good excuse to record the music. I don't know what happened. It was a kind of serendipity. We were all thinking of Gesualdo at the same time.

Gesualdo was an Italian Renaissance composer, a financially independent prince and a count, who murdered his wife and got away with it. Did Gesualdo's life story influence you or inform your interpretation of his music?

Well, I haven't killed my wife [laughs]. Gesualdo was in many ways completely brilliant. He did things that were not done in music for another 300 years. Actually, I think people who have studied music of the Renaissance do realize this. He is not as obscure as one might think. It's just that his music is never performed because it's so difficult. It's unperformable. So getting local musicians to do it was very challenging.

How was it collaborating with the Calliope Chamber Choir and the Jatava Quartet on the Gesualdo recording?

For the Jatava Quartet it was pretty easy. They'd played really hard stuff before. But for the Calliope Choir it was very challenging. In fact the reason I used the string quartet and the choir in many of the compositions as well as other instruments was because for some of this music to be sung a cappella might have been impossible for this group. In the 16th and the 17th centuries it was customary for the different parts in madrigals to be performed either by people or by instruments. It wasn't really specified as much. So I used this idea to sometimes use the instruments to help the singers and also to create different coloristic effects by having different combinations for each piece.

The music features prominently in the scene in which the protagonist Marcus Hammond reveals himself and his inspiration to the final victim. What do you think about how the music is used in the film?

It seems to be used the way the director intended and it seems to work in the way he intended. The whole film is, in a way, the opposite of a Gesualdo piece because the film is frighteningly inexorable. It moves like a really slow steam roller towards a woman who is chained to the pavement. It doesn't stop and it doesn't speed up. It just goes and goes. And the anticipation of crushing this person gets almost unbearable. It's Paul's relentless, unbroken pacing so that the entire film is like one [musical] movement. One arc. This is very unusual. Now, Gesualdo's music is not like that at all because he'll just go for a few bars and then he'll suddenly interrupt it with a completely different thing. In fact, it's the opposite of Paul Spurrier's way of conceiving a work of art. So it's quite interesting that it becomes the metaphor for the art. Outside of that, we talked about the fourth wall a lot. The fourth wall is a visual idea. Basically the character suddenly looks straight into the camera at the audience and this is breaking that wall. But this film breaks that wall in an auditory way. Another instance of that happening is in the film Philadelphia in the scene where Tom Hanks talks about a particular operatic aria. This scene [in Eullenia, in which the protagonist looks into and speaks to the camera] to me is a parallel take on that idea. I don't know many others that are like it. I don't know if Paul was referencing it deliberately.

Can we forget when listening to Gesualdo the fact that the music was composed by a person who did horrible things like murdering his wife?

I would say it's extremely rare for any really, really brilliant person to not have a few dark places. Gesualdo had more than a few, of course. I mean if we stopped listening to every composer who we found morally repugnant we would probably end up not listening to most of the music we listen to. A lot of the time there's a price for genius. Geniuses have shadows. Sometimes their demon comes from an inner dark world. So I would try not to think about the composer as a person. I would rather think about their work. I mean often the very brilliance of their work stems from the darkness of their life. That's the problem. But you can't really perceive it as a separate thing. It's just that that's how the package comes. I am not saying being a creative genius is an excuse to kill your wife. I am just saying it seems to go together pretty often. That's all.

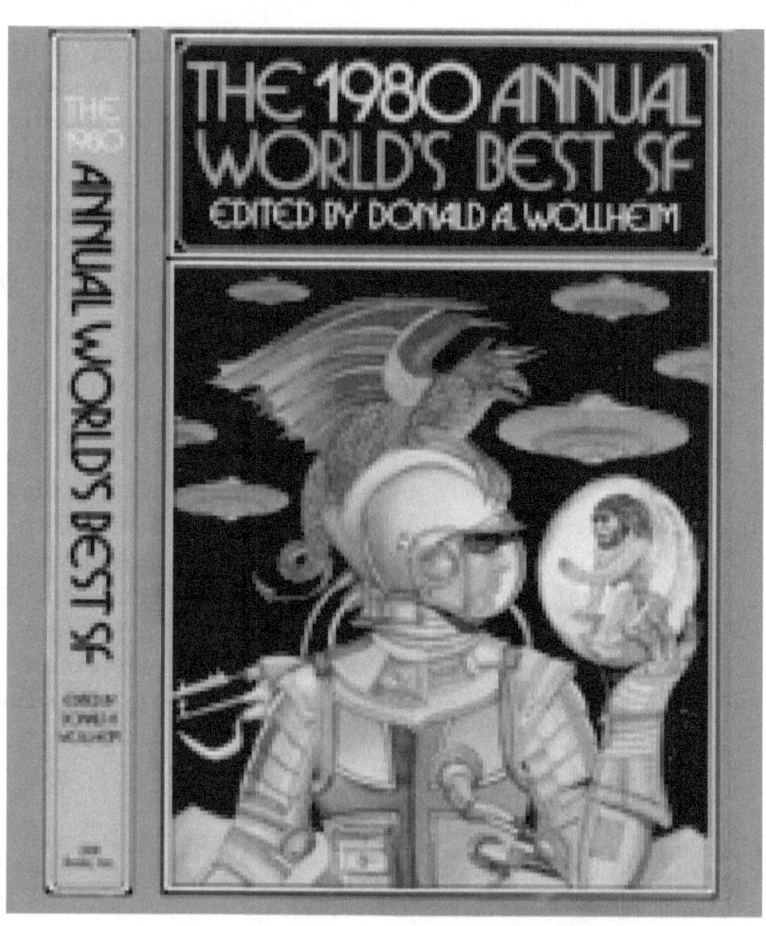

The Thirteenth Utopia was selected for 1980 *World's Best SF.* It narrowly missed a Hugo nomination — by two votes, I believe, on the preliminary ballot.

Lost Tales

The Thirteenth Utopia
by S. P. Somtow

He came to Shtoma in the cadent lightfall, his tachyon bubble breaching the gilt-fringed incandescent clouds like a dark meteor.

Some feelings are never unlearned. Some wonders never fade with experience. So he reflected, Ton Davaryush, master iconoclast, purger of planets, transformer of societies. Especially one — the thrill of power, of potentiality — of a virgin utopia, ripe for the unmasking of its purifying flaw.

Every utopia has its flaw. Ton Davaryush wished it were not so. He was sad — but only for a moment — that he must wreak havoc on this planet, even though it lay at the very limits of the Dispersal of Man; but he had learned not to compromise. With the destruction of twelve deceptive utopias, experience had at least banished misgivings. For Davaryush was two hundred and thirteen years old, and at the height of his analytic powers.

He closed his curiously heavy-lidded eyes to the shimmering of the cloud-banks and the extravagance of the alien landscape that grew constantly as he fell, with its strange sharp-angled trees like gigantic pink spiders, their photosynthesizing pigment having a ferric, not a magnesium base, and its whimsical spiral dwellings of transparent plastic, jutting up at irregular intervals from the blanket of dense vegetation, crimsons and vermilions. He ignored them, and the savage thrashings of the wind as his translucent sphere automatically adjusted to the gravity, softening his fall for landing on Shtoma.

And thought of the covenant: *for the breaking of joy is the beginning of wisdom.* And thought, pathetically: *I, Ton Davaryush, expelled from the mainstream of human society by time dilations and the gulfs of space, am too alone.*

He tried to bury himself — eyes still closed to the atmospheric turmoil — in analyses of what he had been told about this world. How they had fallen into a pattern, an ecological stasis, from which he must release them, whatever the cost. And this was no backward, back-to-nature primitivistic planet, exulting in its own self-conscious apartness and ignorance, but a world whose technical sophistication rivaled his own; exceeded it, in at least one respect, for Shtoma alone, in the entire Dispersal of Man, knew the secret of gravity control. For which they had no use, except for the manufacture of toys. And which they guarded with such miserliness and irrational fervor as to belie their much-vaunted saintliness, their notorious lack of greed, of any other human quality. And the rumor that Shtoma was a utopia was more than could be tolerated.

If it was a utopia it could be destroyed. This he knew. He understood every facet of the utopian heresy. He was a master iconoclast, dedicated to the perpetuation of change. Every utopia has its *flaw*. He clutched this knowledge to him like a secret prayer.

I may be a savior.

He opened his eyes finally. And saw the incredible wildness, the intractable angularity of the landscape, the lurid carmines and scarlets of the trees that lurched toward him with their arachnoid arms outstretched. His bubble slowed itself, gradually, to bring him to the field of rust-colored grass. Alien buzzings and high-pitched song-snatches assailed his ears.

He deactivated his tachyon bubble with a flick of his mind — the keys were cybernetically brain-implanted —and was now at the mercy of the alien environment. At some indeterminate future, he would be rescue — when the thinkhive on the homeworld decided.

I may be a savior. This was more important to him than why they had jealously hidden their secret from a galaxy where knowledge was not for concealing, why they had not used their secret for conquest, as was their right. But this would come. *I am bringing them their human nature, he thought.* The thrill of it lived in his heart. (For this thrill he had joined the Inquest.)

He drew his shimmercloak over his shoulder. It absorbed the fresh air and began to radiate in the safe range, as he knew it would: he stroked it softly as it blushed, pink against the aquamarine fur; wishing, as always, that it was not a dumb semisentient. For he was alone.

Turning in the direction of the nearest habitation, he reviewed once more all he had been told about Shtoma.

A planet unaccountably close to its primary, a white dwarf, yet environmentally anomalous: Earth-sized, temperate, with the wrong atmosphere. With incredible potential for economic power, yet with no armed forces, which ignored the rest of the Dispersal of Man, the galactic authority — leading inexorably to the heretic suspicion of utopia! He began walking. It was not the Inquest's way to arrive conspicuously, gaudy with the trappings of salvation. But then a stranger stood in his path, unmoving. An oldish man, clad severely in a brown tunic; clearly a peasant or slave. He was looking at the ground, and Davaryush had come quite close to him.; The stranger looked up at Davaryush and sang, in a clear tenor, the first alien words he had heard since his arrival, the words:

qithe qithembara
udres a kilima shtoisti

Davaryush signalled to his polyglot implant, then closed his eyes to see, as though inscribed on a white page before him, the words "soul, renounce suffering; you have danced on the face of the sun." It appeared to be a form of greeting. But the strange words, with their opaque and patently sinful meaning, strengthened his suspicions; and he approached the stranger diffidently. There was one other thing experience never banished: fear. Activating his implant so that it would intervene in his speech functions, he said: "I am from another world. Who may I address?"

The alien's gaze chilled him, though it contained no malice. "You are Inquestor Davaryush, of the Clan of Ton. Welcome." Abruptly the stranger beamed and stretched out his arms to embrace Davaryush. The Inquestor yielded ungracefully. He had misjudged; this was no peasant. "We were expecting you."

"Yes. I come to investigate Shtoma's utopian possibilities, so that it may be considered for the honor of being named a Human Sanctuary." Davaryush did not blush at the lie, for it came easily to him by now.

"So! How delightful." His eyes laughed themselves into a hatchwork of wrinkles. "I am your host, Ernad. You must be weary; come."

Who was this man, poorly dressed and without a single attendant, who dared to address a Master Inquestor by name and who knew his mission? Again the alienness of the world unnerved him. The clouds had parted to reveal the white dwarf unnaturally close. The rough wind tousled the grass, blood-red and tall. He started to answer Ernad, but the old man had turned, expecting Davaryush to follow him.

A stony path, pebbled with shiny stones, led to the first recognizably human artifact: a displacement plate, metallic and . incongruous in the middle of the field. He was unprepared for it. He was forced to remind himself that this was no primitive world — in spite of the absence of war or, apparently, slavery.

"When can I begin my investigation? The Inquest must know on in time for the Grand Convocation," he said.

Ernad beckoned Davaryush onto the plate. "Frankly, we have so little involvement with the worlds outside —" he began, then stopped himself. "Well, as you wish; whenever you wish." Davaryush was suspicious of the warmth in his voice, but it appeared convincing. Clearly he was dealing with a master of ambiguity. But the impropriety and unashamedness of "little involvement" compounded his bewilderment.

They materialized in what appeared to be one of the structures he had glimpsed during the landing. He reeled with the vertigo of it—the crazy swirlings and spiralings of transparent walls, the cacophony of chimings and . chirpings that bombarded his senses. How could they live amid such a wilderness of sensual stimuli? Where was their discipline, their culture? A woman nearly ran into him, then trotted away, laughing; children and young people sauntered by, gaily calling out "qithe qithembara; udres a kilima shtoisti!" completely without respect. "You must forgive them," said Ernad, interrupting his dismay. "You are an off-worlder, and...well, it is especially exciting for them now. It is almost time for the festival of initiation, and anything can spark their enthusiasm." He said this matter-of-factly, with no trace of criticism in his voice, again pointing up his alienness.

"They are your attendants?" Surely someone important enough to be his host would have servants of a kind. "No; neighbors, relatives, friends. My house is theirs."

But Davaryush was thinking: what of the initiation ceremony? Perhaps that was the flaw. Perhaps there was some unspeakable rite, some trauma they were all forced to go through ... perhaps this would be the handle he could use to save this misguided people.

"Ernad, I must rest," he said. "But after, I would see everything on your world: your games, your pleasures, your prisons, your criminals, your asylums, your places of execution."

"Ah. Yes, I have heard of madmen and criminals. I am not uneducated, Inquestor Ton," replied Ernad mysteriously. They turned down a corridor of glass that swerved upwards into the air, and Davaryush felt a sudden dislocation, as though he had changed weight or down had become sideways, and he found they were walking upside down, on the ceiling.

"What is happening?"

Ernad laughed mildly. "It is the same principle, you know, as the varigrav coasters. You must have seen them, our principal export—"

"Buy why fool around with gravity inside your dwellings?"

"Why not? Would you not be bored, if all directions remained constantly the same...?"

Up became *down* again. They reached a large chamber that seemed to be perched, precariously, on the point of a translucent pyramid in the sky. "Your resting place. It is my own chamber, Inquestor; I trust you will find it comfortable."

Davaryush's eye alighted on the only adornment of the room; apart from the resting-pad. It was a huge, capelike sheet of some sheer material that hung on one wall, like a rainbow sail, rippling: softly in the ventilating breeze. It was beautiful, he conceded, but bewilderingly complex, uncivilized.

"This cape? What is it for?"

"Oh. My wings," Ernad said.

Davaryush knew then how addicted they must be to the varigrav coasters, those toys they had inflicted on the rest of the galaxy. And he looked at the old man, who seemed utterly disingenuous, and wondered if it were possible that this sincerity were not, after all, the product of a trained deviousness, but merely a product of his lower mentality. For here was a toy, hanging on the wall as though it were a god.

"Leave me, Ernad," he said brusquely.

He was trying to establish authority, the distancing proper for an Inquestor. He needed to preserve his mask of sternness, for he was already sad. He was vulnerable, he realized, even after twelve successful missions.

For he was nothing if not compassionate.

You have compassion, Davaryush.

"Yes, Father." He was twelve years old, veteran of three wars, and now an initiate. And alone, in the small room, with the ~ Inquestor, whose eyes glared fire and millenial wisdom. Now after more than two centuries, the scene returned, vivid.

When you came to kill the condemned criminal, you did not torture him or play with him. as was your right, an essential part of the initiation. You killed him cleanly. in a matter of seconds. slicing him into two congruent parts with your energizer. It was artistically done. But why?

"Father. it was necessary to show skill, not cruelty. I have already killed many people. He feigned an assurance that was far from his true feelings.

Very well. I name you to the Clan of Ton.

Davaryush started, gasped audibly despite his knowledge of roper conduct ... he had come expecting to fail, to be returned to homeworld. The Clan of Ton... that would mean seminary, long lonely years on harsh, inhospitable planets, unwelcome, thankless labor for the sake of pure altruism. "Father—"

You are unworthy. I know. Nevertheless, the Inquest takes what it can get.

His first mission was the planet Gom, a hot planet of a blue-white star. The people lived in tall buildings, thousands to a building, fifteen billion to the planet. But they were happy. They were quite ignorant of their responsibilities as a fallen race; reliant on automata, they pursued their hedonistic existence without regard for their true natures. They suffered from the heresy of utopia.

He remembered how he found the flaw to that utopia. Every year, in a special ceremony marked by compulsive gratifications of the senses, all those over the age of fifty intoxicated themselves and then committed suicide, leaping by thousands into the volcanic lava lakes that boiled ubiquitously on every continent.

He had saved them. Whispering to only one or two: *And what* if you did *not* die? he had created civil wars, revolutions, unhappiness. People ran mad, setting fire to the machines that had succored them. Then the ships of the Inquest came, bringing comfort with them, comfort and truth.

But the happiness had tempted him. *Remember. man is a fallen creature. Davaryush. Utopias exist only in the mind. a state to which it is given us to aspire. But to imagine we have attained that state—that is to deny life. The breaking of joy is the beginning of wisdom.*

Now he was no longer tempted. For he had seen such as the planet Eldereldad, where the happy ones feasted on their own children, which they produced in great litters, by hormonal stimulation; and the planet Xurdeg, his most recent mission. where the people smiled constantly, irritatingly, showing no face except the face of rapt ecstasy, until he finally learned that the penalty for grief was dismemberment, to feed the hungry demands of the degenerating bodies of five-thousand-year-old patriarchs ... yet when he had asked one of these ancients, what he most desired, he had replied: To *feel* grief. But I am *afraid* to die for it.

Ton Alkamathdes, Grand Inquestor of his Sector, who had watched his initiation and had chosen him out for the Clan of Ton, had said to him that day when he was a young boy facin his new destiny: *Never forget the lie. This lie is the sacrifice tho, you must make, the little sin that you must commit, for the saki of saving countless millions. The lie is this: the Inquest is seeking a perfect utopia, a planet that will be designated a Humo Sanctuary, for the edification and glory of the Dispersal of Man.*

You will tell them that always, and always you will understand in your heart that there will exist one tragic flaw.

And always, the ships of the Inquest would follow him. An after, in a year or two, or perhaps a few decades, they would awake to their true natures, and they would fight wars and exhibit avarice and pitilessness, like all the other worlds. Man, is a fallen being.

Remember: you are a guardian of the human condition. He felt the eyes of Ton Alkamathdes on him, even two centuries away and countless parsecs, boring into his soul, purifying him;, and in their sternness he drew a kind of comfort. But then he awoke, long before dawn, and was on Shtoma and frighteningly; alone, exposed to the alien sky under the structures of glass and clear plastics. He found a young girl singing to him, "*qithe qithembara,* Lord Inquestor."

He sat up abruptly, reaching for a nonexistent weapon. "Who; are you?"

"I am Alk, daughter of Ernad." (The voice haunted his:! thoughts for many days, reminding him of the whispering sea on homeworld.) "Will you be pleased with me? Of all the children who saw you, I was most taken by you, Inquestor."

They were depraved, shockingly amoral! They sent their own children to sleep with strangers! "No!" he cried out, and the severity of his own emotion startled them both. "On our worlds we do not do things like this."

"But father said to show you our love, the love of udara." *Udara?* (Their name for the dwarf star, their sun, whispered his polyglot implant. Again he was puzzled.)

"Leave me, please." He tried to exclude the pain from his voice. Shame flooded him. In the starlight he saw disappointment on her face, and thought: they do not even hide their emotions! what savages, what innocents! And without a further word she rose and left him, noiseless as a breeze.

Quickly he ran through what he had learnt in those few hours. They dressed severely, denying all rank and pomp and self-importance; they made curious fetish of their wings, they were morally loose, they did not make any effort to conceal their feelings, but were like children, wholly innocent of the need for tact and diplomacy—and this last thing, the love of *udara*.

That could mean anything. Every perversion, every practIce of perversion was possible, because of the human condition.

And, under the strange constellations, knowing that he had no weapons and that he could not know when he would be rescued, he began to recite the first prayer he had ever learnt. Its meaning, for its language was no longer spoken, was a sublime mystery to the Inquest, but all who went through the seminary could repeat it, as a solace, in times of emotional turmoil. The nonsense words —perhaps little more than gibberish distorted by man's long history — were a kind of bond between the members of the Inquest, all solitary men: *"pater noster, qui es in inferno..."*

"But—what is in these black boxes? I have seen several during my stay here," Davaryush demanded of the heretic priest.

The white-bearded old man — a magnificent mottlement of wrinkles and discolorations, without the common decency of cosmetics — smiled beneficently at him. *"Udara,"* he said. *"Udara* is in them."

"Will you not touch it?" the priest said, beckoning to him. The temple's black box — it was perhaps a meter square — stood in the center of the transparent hall which could have held ten thousand people without any trouble. It was the only object in the chamber. "Come, touch; you will feel *udara*."

Hesitantly, Davaryush went up to it with his hand outstretched. He felt wobbly-kneed, as though his weight were constantly shifting, as though he were losing control of his limbs. Gingerly, he brushed the cool metal with his fingertips.

Overwhelming joy coursed through his thoughts for a moment. He saw homeworld fleetingly, and ached for it, heard the music of the sea, saw vividly the faces of his parents, whom his own time dilation had stranded in an unreachable past ... they smiled at him, he was a child half their height, reaching up to touch their faces, laughing ...

And snatched away his hand as though he had been burnt. This was dangerous, clearly some powerful hallucinogenic device. He stared at his hand in terror.

The happiness he had just felt echoed in his mind. He was tempted to reach out again, and he controlled himself with tremendous difficulty, and knew he had stumbled upon one of the key clues to what was wrong with Shtoma.

They were self-deluders, obviously, intoxicating themselves with false memories and artificially induced joys. "Did you not feel the love of *udara*, stranger?"

"No, priest. I felt — I remembered something I thought I'd lost forever."

He turned to leave. "You do not wish for more? Ah, but you have not danced on the face of the sun."

He turned again, saw the look of pity in the priest's face, the expression of *ah, but you are incapable of understanding.* So he walked hurriedly out, not bothering to acknowledge the priest hearty "*qithe qithembara.*"

Ernad was waiting for him, and the girl Alk, who was — by daylight — a creature of striking beauty, not in her facial features but in the way she moved and spoke; and another of Ernad's children, Eshly, a little boy of about six, who prattled and asked questions as though he were much younger, and was quite devoid of discipline. They walked on to the next displacement plate, Ernad smiling, the girl and her brother running excitedly, then lagging behind, Davaryush moody.

Ernad told him more about the Shtoikitha, the people of the dance (and they called their planet Shtoma, Danceworld.)

"Yes, we're a very thinly populated planet, only half a million souls ... what do we eat? There is fruit in the forests, small animals too, crustacea of fantastical shapes in the rivers; we don't have agriculture here. The fruit of the gruyesh falls to the ground and ripens, and when it turns mauve we tap it for the *zul*, tha mildly fermented sweet juice that you drank this morning..."

"Crime?"

"Why should anyone commit it?" Ernad laughed gently. "We have *udara*, you see, so it isn't necessary."

"I don't understand. My polyglot implant translates that word simply as "sun"; but I have heard it in at least a dozen, meanings since I came to Shtoma. I know that semantics aren't perfect, but could I be missing something? You can't tell me that your people, in all their evident complexity, attribute all your fortunes to some mythical property of your sun!"

Davaryush was exasperated now. It was becoming a strain to maintain his investigator's pose. Clearly the problem on this planet had to do with some fundamental misunderstanding of the workings of the universe.

They had come to a small clearing, having vanished and rematerialized several times: it was level, dotted with pink shrubs ... the two children, or rather the young woman and the boy, had run forward, breathless, and had collapsed, exhausted, on the grass ... *by now, they would both be warriors, in the real world,* he thought. How sad, that they were trapped in a permanent preadolescence.

The boy he felt compassion for: he was like a retarded child who is nevertheless extremely beautiful. But Ernad was talking again.

"Still you don't see, you don't comprehend the elegant simplicity of it. Relax! Feel the singing in the sky: one *cannot* comrnit evil here."

He tried to feel, sensing, in the absurdity of the old man's beliefs, some core of faith that he would never be able to alter ...

The soft susurrant rustlings of the red forests sang to him, but in their singing was mingled, chillingly, an image of homeworld ... he tensed, instinctively, knowing he was playing with fire.

"Have you ever ridden a varigrav coaster?"

"No!" The thought horrified him. Abandonment to the senses, to utter helplessness! Never would he..."It is a pity. What did you feel, when I asked you to listen to the music of *udara?*" (Again, some obscure semantic twist.) "I don't know. A memory. It doesn't matter."

"On the contrary; it probably does matter. But you will learn at the initiation ceremony, perhaps."

"I am to take part?" Nothing would induce him to take part in any barbarian rite! Why, he might be mutilated, he might have to watch some unspeakable evil ... but Ernad smiled the smile that excluded him from those who understood, frustrating him even more. "*Udara* is the key to what you are searching for, you know. Without it, this world would surely not be the paradise it has become."

"Why, that's ridiculous."

The two children of his host had come up and were watching him intently. "Father," said the boy Eshly, "don't be hard on the poor man."

He was so naive, so tactless, so ignorant! But Alk only looked at him, knowing what had passed between them in the night. (He knew now that no stigma was attached to sexual promiscuity; an expression of affection, nothing more. Finally, he had had to concede that this in itself was no flaw.)

"I must show you —" Ernad began.

"Take him to the nearest varigrav coaster, *please*, Father," Eshly cried urgently. He clasped Davaryush's hand — such presumption in a stripling, such undeserved trust — and propelled him toward the nearest displacement plate.

And in an instant they were at the edge of a cliff, sheer and blindingly white, that stretched perhaps half a klomet down to a cleared and endless plain, without the pink of vegetation. The plate where they had arrived stood in the shadow of a tremendously tall column of the transparent building material they used.

It was slender — the width of a few men, and it reached up to vanish somewhere in the vague loftiness of the clouds that hid *udara* from view then. This was nothing like the varigrav coasters he had seen, children's pleasure things. This was overpoweringly stark, and huge, a quasi-religious luminousness emanated from it. Its vastness distorted the scale of everything so he felt a crazy disorientation, while the two children, in nonchalant irreverence, were pushing him to the other side shouting at him to hurry.

"Quick, come, Inquestor!" shouted Eshly. A lift platform was descending for them. Turning to watch the sky beyond the cliff Davaryush saw black dots and smudges, microscopic in the expanse of sky and white plain, and he knew what they were. An ancient fear petrified him, he was like a robot as they buckled him in to the elevator. Suddenly, with a wild jerk, they were aloft racing up to the starting point in the clouds, and the rushing blood in his brain crashed against the rushing of the mad winds. He was nauseated; he closed his eyes and muttered his ancient prayer' longing for an end.

At the top there was a sort of control room, diving platform of various sizes, racks where sets of wings were set out, not the rainbow-colored type that adorned his resting-room, but plaid ones, black or gray. Alk and Eshly each seized a set of wings and had run to the platforms and leapt off the edge while Davaryush, fought a wild impulse to go to their rescue.

He saw them in the air, falling, falling with dizzying speed; and soon they had vanished — and then he saw them again, flung violently upward by the interplay of differing gravity fields, screeching with delight as the varigravs hurled them into!, turbulent whirlpools, and the wind, which was pulled in so many different directions that it was a distended, distorted tornado blasting his ears. He found himself clutching the railings in terror,!he who had seen nine wars.

But the squeals of pleasure became fainter. The two became black dots, joining the rapidly shifting patterns of swirling: specks in the distance. It was more tolerable to look at, pretty patterns against the sky, but when he thought about what was   happening to them (gravity fields wrenching them in different directions, stretching their bodies' tolerance to its very limits,   how could anyone find it pleasurable?) he—"

"Please, take me out of this."

"As you wish."

They went into the control room. They shut out the roaring of the winds and the silence shocked him for a moment, before he gathered his analytic senses enough to look around him...It was an empty room, like all the others he had seen on Shtoma, domed in the standard material, so that *udara* shone relentlessly inside, with a half-dozen of the black boxes predIctably scattered, haphazardly, across the floor.

"I'm impressed." Davaryush tried to sound sincere. "How does it all work, incidentally?" He labored a little over the casual tone of this question, since finding out the secret would make a great difference to the other civilized worlds.

"The scientific principle, or the technical aspects?" Davaryush was startled for a moment by the man's willingness to reveal.

"Both."

"Well, you know as well as I do that gravity control works by selective graviton exchange...the coaster also manufactures antigravitons, which exist of course only with some difficulty under normal conditions."

"But how do you manufacture antigravitons?" Davaryush was excited; uncautiously he let it slip through, was not devious enough in asking the question. Ernad seemed not to be aware of such things.

"I'm simply not a scientist," he said — he did not sound at all as if he was trying to put Davaryush off—" and in any case *udara* controls details like that." He pointed happily to the boxes.

Again the evasive tactics, the semantic deceptions! If the people of Shtoma were able to lie with such easy naturalness, perhaps Shtoma had never been a logical candidate for utopiahood. Perhaps his journey had been wasted.

But the Grand Inquestor had entrusted him, and the Inquest was wise.

He saw the children returning, swung upwards in a golden arc that transected *udara* through the shimmering cloud banks...

"Time to go home. It will be night." Ernad motioned to his guest. "I hope you will feel more comfortable this time, and not be so afraid of the height."

The black boxes glinted in the *udara*-light. They attributed everything to those boxes, Davaryush thought. Was there something in it? Of course not. They were lying to him, creating some enormous joke at his expense.

Walking home through the ruddy terrain, Ernad told him how everybody on Shtoma participated in the initiation ceremonies every five years, almost to a man, because those who been through it once could be renewed, purified.

"You'll understand everything, you know, once you have taken part ... the black boxes, the *udara*-concepts. I know that you find us strange. He chuckled to himself, then added earnestly, "You will take part, won't you?"

Slowly, with the realization that he might well be falling a trap, a trap cleverly constructed upon his own curiosity and the necessities of his mission, he said: "I have no choice." For mission was to understand, and after understanding to co Even now, compassion touched him, more than ever before.

The accident happened.

Eshly, the boy, had run on ahead to the next plate. He tripped and stumbled, face down, and the power surged. They were upon him, the resounding clang echoing in the woods The three of them knelt down by the plate.

He lay like a discarded toy. The displacement field aborted — it was an accident that practically never occurred, almost unthinkable — and had wrenched half his body away then slung it back in a nanosecond, so that he was in one but impossibly bent.

Davaryush waited for the tears, for the signs of grief. But only sighing was the breeze and the voices of the alien Lightfall was ending.

"Go on, Alk," Ernad whispered to his daughter, "the others will want to know." His voice was icy calm.

Davaryush stood to follow as he lifted up the corpse, seemed merely asleep until one saw the inhuman angle of arms, and carried it into the encroaching forest, and returned without it, with the red shadows darkening him. There seemed to be no sadness in his face. Indeed, he almost smiled. Was this some incredible fortitude, even in the face of an impossible tragedy? Davaryush devoured the man with his eyes, seeking: some clue to his emotions. And he thought, I have found the *flaw*.

And now it was time to plant the doubt, because the lowest point in a man's being is also the beginning of his ascent. Davaryush thought bitterly: here is a people that blithely throws the bodies of its sons into the forests to rot, that has forgotten grief that does not value human life at all. Here was the flaw.

Davaryush tried to put a lot of anger into his voice, to exclude compassion while not striving too much for an oracular effect: "You don't care about your child," he said. "Love is not part of your utopia, is it? Humanity is what you have abandoned, isn't it?" *Now you are going to break down. Now your repressed humanity will come rushing to the surface.* It had happened twelve times before, and countless other times with other Inquestors.

Ernad did not collapse. He stared at Davaryush with unmitigated pity.

"Of course I grieve for him. I am desolate, Davaryush. But you do not understand our perspectives, or our overview of life.

"With renewal my grief will be cleansed. And I grieve for him most, that he did not live to dance on the face of the sun."

And Davaryush knew that he had understood nothing at all, nothing. Never had he felt so palpably the alienness of this world, the total incommunicableness of it. His mind whirled in a wild kaleidoscope of images: strange winds, blood-crimson forests with spider arms, flagrantly immodest buildings open to the elements, a dead child unmourned, a dead child who had been playing games amidst the incomprehensible forces of black boxes that manipulated gravity fields ... and this strange man's face, which should be racked with sorrow, yet insulted him with an unwanted pity. *I wish I could kill him.*

The death-impulse rose in him, a monster of the subconscious, and he suppressed it with a superhuman effort. *He is a product of his misguided culture, not to be blamed,* he reminded himself. *I have come to save him; I must never forget that; even if I cause his death, I come as a savior.*

He had miscalculated again. Thinking to elicit from the stranger his hidden guilt, his dormant human responses, he had instead forced his own desire to kill to the surface. This desire should long have been dead, since he had renounced it for the sake of the salvation of the Dispersal of Man; yet it haunted him still, a spectre from the buried past. Perhaps the will of the man was stronger than his ...

At last he found he could feel a bond between himself and the alien, in this moment of deepest misunderstanding. For they were both men, both fallen beings.

"Ernad," said Davaryush, "I pity you." The two of them walked, through the miscolored landscape, up to the twisted house.

Asleep that night, he was nine years old, celebrating the end of his first war.

And they came to Alykh, the pleasure planet. He and Tymyon and Ayulla and Kyg and the other companions, losing themselves in the cacophony of the crowds.

"Wait till you see *this!*" Kyg shouted, and she leapt on to the plate like a cat. They disappeared —

And Davaryush saw it, a topless tower of brick and and concrete and plastic and sparkling amethysts, studding walls like jewelled knuckle-dusters...

"What is it?"

"Daavye, don't you know anything?" Tymyon cackled offensively.

Kyg said, with mock primness: "It's a...VARIGRAV COASTER!"

The tower glinted oddly, catching the sunset. "Look," Kyg impatiently, "you dive off the top, you see, and it sets action a series of random gravity-field interferences, and you plummet like a hawk and you float upward and you swing dangerously and you curve and then you land where you started, like a feather."

("It's beautiful" whispered Ayulla the silent.)

"Well, let's go!" Tymyon and Kyg raced each other to the tower, and the crowds were everywhere, aliens, child-warrior brandishing their weapons, pimps, crusader-flagellant Inquestors and their retinues, slave-hunters, veiled Whispershadows from the borders of the Dispersal, dirty children strumming on dreamharps, dissonant alien musics, and an itinerant space opera howling full-blast through amplification jewels, and Davaryush was spellbound, unmoving.

He had never ...

The tower held him.

And the little specks that were people, dust-motes in violet sunset.

"Aren't you coming?" Ayulla's voice was almost lost in confusion.

"No." He was petrified.

"Come *on!* They're all the rage now, all the way from Shtoma you know, from the limits of the Dispersal..."

"No! No!" (It was said that the greatest thrill, when you fell, was the very certainty of death, suddenly averted by a twist the field. At the moment of inevitable doom, it was said, you felt so *alive.)*

Ayulla was laughing at him. "How many people have you killed, Daavye? How can you be so scared of *life?"*

(He was ashamed. He resolved, then, to change his circle of friends.)

Now wake up. Face the hostile planet.

He moved, murmuring "Homeworld." Shrill cries of children awakened him. And then Alk was at the entrance to his room: "Initiation, Inquestor; hurry."

He threw on his shimmercloak. It tightened around him, sensing his need for warmth, though it was not cold.

The wings on the walls had gone.

The whole family, a dozen or more of them, trooped without ceremony into his room, heady exhilaration in their faces. Quickly he followed them outside, struggling to keep up with them. His heart had sunk when he saw that the wings had vanished. For he had an inkling, now, of what this rite must involve, and it terrified him.

Many displacements later, they were on a mountaintop overlooking a vast plain that glittered silver-gray with a thousand spaceships. The ships littered the fields, end to end so that the red grass was quite covered, all the way to the horizon...he could not imagine what they were for. Shtoma had hardly any commerce with other worlds.

Isn't it breathtaking?" Alk grasped his arm, and he felt himself shivering...

"How many of them are there, Ernad?" he said, wonderingly. This ceremony involved a journey, it seemed; perhaps on some satellite, some other planet.

The children were dancing and tugging at him and hollering in circles round him, and Ernad did not seem disposed to answer his questions. "Come," he said, and after another displacement they were at the entrance to a ship. (It was much as he knew them; ships did not differ much, having been perfected many millennia ago, before the Dispersal.) But the number of them! And the mobs of people, their wings tucked under the arms, giggling, chattering away as they climbed into them!

In the mid-distance, some of them had already risen. They rose at even intervals, in perfect order, and he could see a long chain of them stretching into the sky, where they glittered like a jewelled necklace in the early lightfall. Quickly (almost shamefacedly) he stifled his wonder, for he knew he must analyze everything, if he was to solve the most taxing problem of his life, the enigma of Shtoma. So he climbed the steep steps into the belly of the ship.

It was only a small cruiser, built for perhaps five hundred; there must be a thousand of them, then, to hold the whole population of Shtoma. It was impersonal, gray-walled like every ship; and it appeared to be a short-hauler, so Davaryush knew they Were not going off-system. People were filing into their chambers, seeming to know exactly where they belonged, Davaryush stood stupidly for a few moments before Alk came for him, and took him to the family's cabin.

After a while, he felt the noiseless lifting of the ship.

Some time later Ernad led him to the viewroom, screens afforded an unobstructed three hundred and degree view of space; and he saw how the line of ships behind and before, each an exact distance from the other, links a metal serpent of space...he asked Ernad where they going.

"To *udara*, of course!"

The old man looked blankly at "Not seriously."

"Are there any other planets in this system? Any moons? are not a mendacious people, Davaryush; perhaps that has occurred to you yet." He spoke patiently, as though reproving favorite child, and the attitude stung Davaryush.

He turned to see, on the other side of the room, that *udara* had swollen and was a blindingly white flame ball against blackness. He knew by now that when the word *udara* came he would get nowhere; so he tried something else. The ubiquitous black boxes were everywhere; in the viewroom they were stacked neatly in the middle of the floor.

"Those *udara*-boxes: they power the ship perhaps?" he only half-skeptical.

Ernad laughed again, enjoying his guest's ignorance. (Again Davaryush felt a bitter hate, a death-lust, for his host). "Not all; they are quite empty, and our spaceships work in the. normal way."

After a moment, he said: "Now look, Inquestor: they are darkening the screen otherwise *udara* would become unbearable."

"How can you say we are going there?"

"Just look at the face of the sun. There, look."

Udara was growing rapidly, and Davaryush saw: "There's a black spot on the sun's surface!"

"*That's* where we are going."

The black dot was perfectly round. This was impossible. "It must be artificial!" he gasped. These people, far from being simple utopians, were capable of galaxy-dominating technological feats!

"Artificial? In a manner of speaking." Then he explained, "The dot of course is only black by comparison, obviously; when we get there it will appear white and incandescent."

The screen was cut in half! One side was completely black, the other painfully bright, and there were white flame-tongues that shot up, a hundred kilometers high. They were approaching the sun's atmosphere; in its heart, Davaryush knew, matter was packed into inconceivable density.

"And now...there are tablets you must take, since you will not be able to breathe for a few hours; they will release oxygen into your bloodstream."

"What do you mean?"

"You're going to jump into the sun."

Davaryush understood now. They had led him on, and all the time were preparing this elaborate fiery execution. "I'll vaporize instantly!" he said.

"You don't understand, do you?" Ernad countered with surprising vehemence. "Gravity is under control, heat is under control! This is no ordinary star, this is *udara*. Every five years, we all ride on the gravity-fields here, and become clean...

Davaryush's mind reeled under the impact of this revelation. The sun filled the screen completely now, unbelievably white ..."You mean that you *built* this star? You built a varigrav coaster . on the surface of a sun?"

"If only we had the technology!" Ernad smiled a little. "Why, the mind boggles. You are so close to the answer, and yet so far, so incredibly far! Well, we are all bound by the limits of our experience. It is time to live; explanations will follow."

They were in the airlock, then; waves of nausea crashed in his head, and he stood stock-still like a martyr waiting for death (which he felt himself to be) while they put the wings on him and the tittering of the children pelted his brain like painful hailpellets —

The airlock opened! There was whiteness, such whiteness. He shut his eyes and fell. Fell. Fell. His blood was burning. He was burning, he was falling into hell, plummeting helplessly into the scorchswift firebreath of the sunwind. He screamed, he thrashed his body uselessly against emptiness, he opened his eyes and the whiteness shattered his vision, the featureless whiteness, so he screamed and screamed, until he was no longer aware of his screaming.

He heard voices out of the past (*Kill the criminal Daavye no I can't I can't you have compassion my son compassion man is a fallen being*).

He reached the limit of his falling. And soared! And was flung upwards, upwards, on an antigraviton tide! And swerved, and fell headlong again, and swooped in tandem with a tongue of flame, and his scream was a whisper in the thunder of the wind (*come on Daavye you fool it's the latest craze no! are you afraid of life or something Daavye Daavye?*) and fell and fell (*pater noster qui es in inferno*) and fell ...

And soared! And caromed into the roaring flame! And fem And saw death, suddenly, and came face to face with himself, and knew death intimately ... and fell

(Kill the criminal Daavye compassion compassion) and fell ...

Trust me.

Falling, the voice embraced him. The voice sang through him:, The voice made him tingle like a perfect harp-string, dispelling his terror in a moment. He was a nothing touched by love. *(Memories came like endless printouts but there was one memory on the verge of crystallizing, and he was waiting for it, waiting for it to come, clear as a presence —)*

The voice was like homeworld. The roaring was the whisper of the sea. He could almost see his parents again: and fell and fell ...

... and was touched by love and fell and lost consciousness;, becoming one with an ineffable serenity.

"Answers! I want answers!"

He woke, sweating, in the room in the twisted house. Ernad was there, and the whole family; he felt their concern, and then he broke down and sobbed violently," hopelessly.

"I think we deserve some answers too, Ton Davaryush," Ernad said softly; there was iron in his gentleness. (He heard the others whispering among themselves: "When he came back to the ship, he was in a trance, unconscious."

"He's been like this for weeks."

"Now understand this, Davaryush," said Ernad, "you are not the first Inquestor to visit our planet. And will not be the last either."

Davaryush did what he never dreamed he would do: between fits of weeping, he told them the whole story, how he had come to Shtoma to save the people from themselves, how he had been defeated, how he understood nothing now, nothing at all.

(They fed him with sweet *zul* and were so kind to him. This, too, evoked a strange wonder and respect in him; for he had wanted to betray them.)

"Well, you were promised an explanation. Listen, then: *Udara* is no ordinary star. Of course we didn't build him: that's ridiculous. But — do you know anything about the origins of sentience? Well, you know how life evolves: how certain arrangements of atoms, certain paradigms, created purely by chance interactions, you understand, becoming living beings, self-aware, sometimes ... white dwarfs are created by incredible cataclysms, by a star going nova, dying ... somehow, a spark of life was made, after the nova, and *udara* became self-aware. *Udara* is alive, Davaryush! and we have acquired a symbiotic relationship with him that permits us to exist in the scientifically anomalous state ... do you follow? In the black boxes, Davaryush: pieces of the sun."

Davaryush lay back, stupefied, his thought fired by the incredible imagery of it. "Did you imagine that mere people such as we could create and uncreate gravitons and anti-gravitons? How much power is available, without the resources of a star? Could we make and unmake gravitational fields? Could we dim the sunlight on one area of the sun, so as to be unharmed by its heat? *Udara* does this, by his own will; his knowledge of physical laws is several orders beyond our understanding. We think that he is aware of himself, not only in this four-dimensional continuum, but also in other continua."

"But with this power," Davaryush said, "with this sun to do your bidding, can't you conquer the galaxy, win wars?"

"You still don't understand! The sun does not do our bidding; the sun does all this because he *loves* us." (Davaryush remembered, suddenly, how love had touched him when he was plummeting towards death.) "You felt it in the sunlight. You would always have felt it, but you were so full of confusion and contradiction, and so many people had lied to you...but when you fell into the sun, when you danced on the sun's face, then you understood. You see, we can't commit evil, because in the act of dancing — what the rest of humanity thinks of as our little children's game — we have partaken of a tiny fragment of his nature..."

But let me plant a doubt in your mind. That is what you came to do to us, isn't it? Well: what if the Inquest existed, not for salvation, but for destruction? What if its sole purpose were to perpetuate its leaders' desire for conquest, and its mouthpieces, the "Inquestors," were simply indoctrinated with pseudo-religiousness to make them more fanatical, more serviceable?"

And Davaryush knew that he had lost his faith. (He wondered what answer he would give them about Shtoma. It would probably be unsatisfactory; they would undoubtedly have to send another Inquestor. But he no longer cared what the Inquest thought.)

Finally there came a day when Alk came running in to him, breathlessly: "Your tachyon bubble, it's hovering above the house!" He stepped outside. The sun shone on him, bathing him with inexpressible joy. Suddenly the memory came to him, the memory that was just beginning to come to him, before he became unconscious —

He was six years old. The ship was waiting to take him to the war. He was standing there with his father, by the sea shore, and his father seized him, on impulse, and threw him into the air, an he screamed for help, half-laughing, and fell f~r an eternity, in{ the arms that were for him, for protecting him, for loving him:; At last he understood the love of *udara* .

...But the children of the house had come and were clustere around him, making much of him, and Ernad stood at th entrance, waving to him. I

"*Qithe qithembara!*" he yelled frantically, forcing back his tears

He took one more step towards the bubble.

You have danced on the face of the sun.

-Arlington, 1978;

This month, my new opera *Helena Citrónová* came out. It is inspired by the true story of a Slovak Jew in Auschwitz who had a searing, intense relationshipp with an SS-Man. This is the reason I've been a little slow bringing out more episodes of *Homeworld of the Heart*. Now, though, I have a little more time.

My Approach to Musical Language in *Helena Citrónová*

S.P. Somtow

This opera began years ago with an overture: a clanging, elemental, shrieking, painful overture that's not so much like "music" as like the actual sound of a nightmare train.

At that point, I had written a libretto for *Helena,* and I had left it untouched for a year. Helena's story had spoken to me during the course of the BBC interview she gave for their landmark Auschwitz documentary. It wouldn't leave my mind, even though nothing could be farther from my personal experiences as the horror that gripped Central Europe in the 1940s.

I think that when critics describe my operas, they tend to say they're tuneful, filled with exotic coloration and "oriental fragrances." *Helena* is not very much like these descriptions. It is dark. It is terse. And it is full of things left unsaid, emotions too powerful for words, so that the orchestra must be the one to articulate these feelings.

In searching for the musical language to tell this story, I started with a proposition: *What does Europe in the 1940s* sound *like?* and immediately came up with a basic dualism. In previous eras of western musical history, there is a language continuum between the popular and "high art". Works like *The Magic Flute* show clearly that "pop" music could also be imbued with the intellectual appurtenances of "serious" music. In the nineteenth century, stevedores hummed Verdi tunes. Even at the beginning of the twentieth, Mahler can still interweave a snatch of klezmer into a symphonic argument. Then — unique in the history of western music — there is a fracture. This could be about the collapse of tonality, the collapse of multi-ethnic empire states, or some kind of general Zeitgeist — but by the middle of the century, we're looking at two musical states that seem worlds apart. On the one hand the world of coffee house music, swing, Latin and other genres, on the other increasingly esoteric worlds of serialism, extreme virtuosity of rhythmic and harmonic language, new systems of musical thought.

The music of *Helena* is grounded in this duality, starting with the "Helena tone row" that is played when

Helena is first seen coming off the Slovakia transport, and which ends up worming its way into every texture of the opera's musical dialectic. When Helena utters her name, Oscar tells her she has no name, only a number.

I use serial technique in a way as a stand-in for the Nazi world-view — the idea of reducing people to numbers, to a mechanistic vision of people predestined to inferiority by an accident of DNA. Yet every time the row appears, and it does so in a multitude of forms, all the retrogrades and inversions one used to have to learn about in composition lessons in the 1970s, and often multiple forms woven on top of one another — it's accompanied by sustained and aggressively tonal triads, indeed you could call them "pop chords" — which negate the very idea of serialism — which is to escape tonality.

What this tells us is that no matter how much we try to twist Helena into a set of numbers, she won't be so constrained. No matter how many mathematical games you try to play, her humanity surges underneath. In a nutshell, this dichotomy is the heart of the opera.

The "Helena tone row" takes over more and more of the fabric of the opera, and the more it permutates using the traditional serial tropes of inversion and retrograde, the more insistently "pop" the underlying triads become.

At the other pole, a simple triad-based figure is used to represent the relentless turning of the wheels of the Slovakia transport, a nightmare train ride. It's first presented with the entire string section *and* timpani in startling unison from which they do not diverge for page after page of nightmarish, driving music. This theme, too, weaves itself into every aspect of the score.

Viewed as whole, then, the musical language of *Helena* can be seen as a tug of war between extremes of constraint: the permutations of a tone row and the limitations of an unchanging triad.

But this is not the only musical polarity *Helena* toys with. Perhaps one of the more "shocking" uses of musical allusion occurred because I noticed that the Nazi anthem, the *Horst Wessel Song,* could be made to fit on top of Schubert's celebrated song about the nature of music, *An die Musik.* This prompted me to make one of the only significant changes in the story as it unfolded in my researches.

What actually happened, according to sources, was that Helena was made to sing *Happy Birthday* for Franz Wunsch ... and somehow, in that moment, he fell in love with her. I've embroidered the incident a little bit. Although she has been brought to the party to sing a birthday song, one of the guards begins playing the opening to *An die Musik* on the battered piano on stage. Helena realizes that she knows this song and, tentatively at first, she begins to sing it. Franz is riveted. While *An die Musik* is initiated on the out-of-tune onstage piano, it slowly seeps into the orchestral piano amid a dreamlike cloud of dissonant chords.

When Franz later sings of his love, the melodies of *An die Musik* and the Nazi anthem become hopelessly entwined and my message is that the fabric that created the highest cultural aspirations of German culture is also the raw material of its darkest hour.

Numerous other polarities, large and small create the boundaries of the opera's sound-world. From the conflict of major piled on minor (the opera ends in both A flat major and G sharp minor, neither willing to resolve into the other) to the popular musics — tango, klezmer, waltz — that are interwoven with violent atonalities, this opera's world exists at the confluence of clashing extremes.

Having created a libretto which rarely deviates from fragments of the story as gleaned from the interviews and a few articles, I had to create a love story in which the lovers can never be alone together and in which they can't really have a conventional love duet. Yet there are three passages which from an operatic standpoint would seem to be "love duets." The first takes place in a crowd scene of mayhem when Franz has just managed to rescue Helena's bewildered sister from the gas chamber. Publicly he must appear to despise her even as he's trying to tell her he loves her, and she is trying to tell him she can never say that she loves him. Unpacking the syntax of the libretto, you can see that they are not confessing their love to each other, but music tells us they are. The second duet takes place when they are not even in the same room – it is two simultaneous soliloquies where the words, close in form but opposite in intent, coalesce to make a love duet that the lovers are unaware they are singing. The final scene of the opera, an extended epilogue, is one that never happened but can be seen almost as a fantasy sequence; it shows Helena approaching Franz's home in Vienna as though to rekindle the relationship, then realizing that it cannot be, turning around and walking away. Here, she stands outside and does not see him; he looks out of the window and sees her, but she never knows — or never acknowledges that she knows. And from this non-meeting comes the third love duet, one in which the possibility of "normal" intimacy is finally within reach, yet is forever beyond reach. An emotionally charged "love theme" first heard at the beginning of the second act dissipates into a trite waltz played by a coffee-house band, ironically the same musicians who comprised the prison orchestra in the concentration camp scenes, playing polkas and tangos while their fellow inmates were being murdered.

I wanted to ask difficult questions in this opera. I want to tell neither the story of a heroic love set against an unspeakable evil, nor the story of people using each other as love-fantasy-surrogates as a way to survive the unsurvivable. Surely those are both stories that someone else could tell. I do want to consider the question of what love really is, and what redemption really means. I want to consider how someone can hold on to their humanity when someone else tries to strip away everything that makes them human. It was the need to answer these questions that dictated the language of musical polarities in which the opera is composed.

For these polarities reflect the way people would like to see these events — in absolute terms such as good versus evil, madness versus sanity. But reality always contradicts our desire to reduce the narrative to black and white. At the opera's most extreme moments, words invariably fail and the orchestra alone speaks. Unfiltered by the innate deceptiveness of human language, it is the music that delivers the ambiguous truth.

Helena's Journey

— an essay I wrote about Helena for Thai Enquirer

Some years ago, when the Terminal 21 shopping center was new, I spotted a statue of Adolf Hitler in front a clothing store, dressed to look like Ronald McDonald. Around the same time, I learned that there had once been a restaurant called *Hitler Fried Chicken* in Ubon Rachatani. And that nice young college men and women were dressing up in Nazi gear for school parades. It led me to ask some of my students if they knew whether Thailand won or lost the Second World War.

They didn't know.

It was really this that led me to work with embassies in Thailand — Israel, Germany, Austria, Czechia, and others — to try to put on performances that would help teach the reality of what, supposedly, "everyone" knows — but which, it seems, they do not.

The journey of Helena Citronóvá was far more torturous. From the hellish Slovakia Transport to the extermination camps, to an intense, morally ambiguous relationship with an SS-man, to a death march, to being a refugee fleeing to Israel across a devastated post-war landscape, hers was a life that beggared belief — not just that she lived it, but that she survived it.

Hearing her speaking, years later, in a matter-of-fact, collected voice, about these horrors, in an interview in the BBC's landmark Auschwitz documentary, was profound.

It's not that I had not thought about Auschwitz ever before. I knew about it from school. I've had vivid nightmares about Auschwitz all my life, every few years. For me, though Auschwitz was an icon — the central mystery, the central trauma of the twentieth century. Six million is a vast number, incomprehensible in human terms.

Helena was not one of the six million slain — she was one who survived. Yet while six million is a number, *one* is a person. In hearing her story I understood that there were six million separate, individual stories about human beings. There was not one of those six million who didn't want to live. Somehow, she did. It was a story of a person who, no matter what, kept her personhood intact. I don't know if this was what redeemed the SS-man, Franz Wunsch. I don't know where the truth falls, between the two extremes of an idealized love between opposites —or a desperate transactional relationship between two people trying to cling to an illusion of normalcy in a world gone mad. We will never know this because we'll never know what either of them was thinking.

An opera is not about reality. No one walks around singing with a symphony orchestra backing them up. But opera *is* about truth. I composed this opera because the truth haunted and tormented me. Many of my friends hope this opera will "teach people about the Holocaust". I hope so too, but I also hope that the past will teach us about ourselves, and about the earnest longing in all of us for a better, more compassionate world.

Mikey Jiraros

Despatches from Earth
Forty-Two Years with the Force
S.P. Somtow

A long time ago ... and the galaxy might as well be far, far, away because I'm not a quantum particle and so my consciousness is stuck for ever on a swath of spacetime that moves inexorably in one direction only ... it was the opening day of a move called *Star Wars.* Memorial Day, 1977 — and just as with all the other world-shaking events such as the Kennedy Assassination or Pearl Harbor — I'll never forget where I was that day.

The entire Washington Science Fiction Association, a collection of nerds, social misfits, outcasts and other such geniuses, had completely taken over the Uptown Theater, one of the few real movie theaters not yet transformed into a shopping mall tube. Expectations were high. The movie began and the cheering and clapping (and the occasional boo, as when the script didn't seem to know what a *parsec* was) hardly stopped. We loved it, and went on to see it ten, twenty, a hundred times, but even then we knew we had been present at the birth of a new era.

Phrases from the movie entered the language quickly. "These aren't the droids you're looking for" and "Let the Wookie win" were on everyone's lips and still are. Arguably, more lines from this film are in common use today than lines from *Hamlet.* Though the movie was really a recreation of serials from decades back which in turn derived from swashbuckling space opera of the 1930s, a lot about the film was new. It had a strong female character. It had wisecracks. In any age where Japanese culture was starting to invade, its plot was a clever re-imagining of Kurosawa's film *Hidden Fortress* — take *that*, Mr. *Throne of Blood!* It had a cool quasi-religious new-age semi-Zen theory of *everything*.

And its subversion of all we knew actually started with the very first words. A *long time ago* is not how science fiction stories are supposed to begin. They are supposed to be *A very long time from now....* You see, *Star Wars* was saying that science fiction *is* mythology. In a world where there is no commonly held religious worldview, *science fiction* was the source of our myths. Starships and alien princesses were our Jungian collective unconscious.

Thus it was that a low-budget film — one in which, I must remind you, Darth Vader was *never intended to be Luke's father* and in which Han Solo was mean enough to *shoot first* — actually changed how the entire world seems almost everything.

As a composer who had hit an appalling composer's block, was living in Washington and wholly dependent on income from ghost-writing fake nineteenth century symphonies for a humming millionaire, I too was about to experience *total change.* Within a week or so of watching this film, I had sold a science fiction story to a small magazine in Boston.

Just four years later, I was sitting at the Hugo Awards Ceremony, having been nominated for the John W. Campbell Award for "Best New Writer." A few feet away was Gary Kurtz, the producer of *The Empire Strikes Back*, who was also being nominated for a Hugo. We both won.

So, I've lived with these movies a long time.

There was a rumor (after the success of *Empire*) that this would be part of a gargantuan ennealogy. (I was going to say *nonology,* which is an amusing nonce word, but the pedant in me rebelled.) But it did not happen. Not the way we all thought, anyway.   And yet, on Saturday, I bestirred myself and went to the Emprivé Cinema in Bangkok to see what was billed as the ninth and final installment of the trilogy of trilogies.

I am forty-two years older now. My musician's block broke and I ended up having to juggle a music and a writing career.   I left America and returned to my "roots" — if you could call it that since I actually left Thailand at the age of six months.

The theater in Bangkok is the polar opposite of the Uptown. Sofas with blankets and back-leaning controls and footrests, a reception area with a buffet spread, obsequious staff instead of gangly school kids ... all for less than the cost of a nacho-stained hard fold-down seat in Los Angeles. But movie theaters here have to do *something* to rouse Bangkok audiences from Netflix. Sound is more vibrant, colors are more striking, and every scene of the movie is packed with more *stuff* than one could have dreamed possible in 1977.

I'm now going to review the entire thing. I'll start at the beginning — the *real* beginning, guys, because it is *really* important to understand that sequels and prequels were furthest from people's minds — let alone global phenomena.

So. For many of us, it's really just the first two films that are *classic* in an absolute sense. And the first film — I still hate the title *A New Hope* because this film is actually just *Star Wars,* no sequels, no prequels — is the *only* one that can be considered as a completed arc of a film in its own right). By now, everyone knows that on a deep level it's a deconstruction of *Hidden Fortress.* From the sharp-tongued princess to the two funny sidekicks to the final attack run, the parallelism is a little bit tongue in cheek but it's an early salvo in what would become a wholesale invasion of Asia into the world of American pop culture.

We loved this film because of the adventure but also because it didn't take itself seriously. It wasn't people looking at popular culture and trying to exploit it — it was popular culture in the process of being born. The most beautiful thing about it for science fiction lovers was seeing things we had imagined from geekish childhoods steeped in worlds of imagination. Double sunsets, hyper-jumps, and sweeping through the galaxy while wearing a karate uniform, and evil that actually *looks* evil.

If you asked almost any *real* fan, they will tend to tell you *Empire* is their favorite. It has the great Leigh Brackett — a legendary writer from the "Golden Age" on the screenplay as well as Lawrence Kasdan, as steeped in "Hollywoodness" as Brackett was in the science fiction aesthetic. Irvin Kershner, a surprising directorial choice, brought genuine character development to the film. What surprised *everyone*, after the sunny tone of the first film, was there was darkness here.

Many people assume that Darth Vader's theme was always there, but actually that key-bending *marche militaire* starts in *Empire*. John Williams so defines the nature of Vader that we hear the theme in our minds even when he appears in the first film with different music — the leitmotivic equivalent of retconning.

Darkness was in Luke himself as well — because he never had the sunny, innocent smile again — due, I'm told, to a car crash and surgery that slightly altered his face. Unfortunate as the accident may have been, it lent our perception of Mark Hamill more depth. Lost in the dazzlement at a huge effects scene being shot entirely against a *white* snow background was the fact that

Luke's mauling by a wampa was probably something to do with explaining why he looked a little different.

With the prospect of sequels — perhaps *many* — retrofitting began in earnest. Darth Vader became Luke's father, meaning that Alec Guinness's narration in *Star Wars* would have to undergo a bit of "tweaking". Oh! and that incipient love triangle between Han, Luke and Leia — obviously all that had to be retconned wholesale. But no one minded. In fact, this kind of wild, improvisatory backstory on the fly was a lot of fun.

If there was an inkling of a Zen agenda in *Star Wars,* Yoda as a diminutive grand master made it front and center. The "father" revelation became another iconic moment. The Joseph Campbell, et all, bits were much appreciated as well — the quest in which the hero must ultimately defeat his shadow-self reminded us that everyone in Hollywood has *Hero with a Thousand Faces* and *Golden Bough* and *Archetypes and the Collective Unconscious* on their shelf somewhere — even if just to skim through for ideas.

The weaknesses of *Empire* really only stem from its being the middle of a trilogy — always the hardest to get a handle on, like a middle sibling. And while everyone complains about Boba Fett's truncated role, mostly it was because the toy was so cool-looking and everyone assumed it would be a major role.

Now, I must say that after raving about *Empire,* I found that *Return* (or *Revenge* as we had known it for ages before they chickened out for a more innocuous title) was a tad annoying — everyone had gone over to the Toy Side of the Force. The Ewoks were irritating and, to the anthropologist in me, even a little racist. (Not against mini-teddies, but against real-life stone age cultures that survive today.) But okay. It's a guilty pleasure.

The controversy over the "real face" of Darth Vader was fueled mostly by David Prowse's disgruntlement. This guy really wanted to take off the mask and show people what he really looked like, only to have someone else's face being substituted at the end.

Of course, tinkering with the faces of force ghosts continued, because just when we thought it was safe to go back in the water, the prequel trilogy happened.

Now, for those weaned on the first three films, the prequels were pretty *meh*. For one thing, none of them had the delicate touch of the first film or even the first two sequels. They laid it on with a heavy hand; they were portentous; they were self-consciously *big;* they didn't have witty dialogue; and they were seriously handicapped by having a future already preordained by the existing trilogy.

And bloated. George Lucas is indeed a genius in many ways, but creating an entire science fiction universe with consistency and logic is not one of those ways. He is not Herbert and he is not Asimov — though *Dune* permeates Tatooine and Coruscant is clearly Trantor.

The series was always about a lot of cool things, not about how those cool things *worked*. We didn't care about the logic in the 1970s. We had long forgiven the Kessel Run parsec gaffe, and yet somehow getting all the pieces to fit seemed to matter a lot; an elaborate "just kidding" excuse was found to somehow shoehorn the slip-up into a veneer of science. Why bother? There's virtually no science in *Star Wars* anyway. It's all actually magic with a gloss of technospeak.

The magic was not served well when the technospeak veered from the plausible. Midichlorians were a feature of Madeleine L'Engle's *Wrinkle in Time* series. Now it must be said that this series isn't really science fiction at all — it's basically a religious allegory using the tropes of fantasy and science fiction — a sort of American *Narnia*. Now, to *first* say that the Force is an energy that surrounds everything in the universe, and *then* to say that it's a bunch of one-celled intelligent organisms, is *not* the same as saying light is both a wave and a particle. It's more like translating religious incantations into plain English and realizing that they are mumbo jumbo.

So, having this great need for some kind of plausibility that is not supported by the kind of depth of knowledge that could create such plausibility is one of the problems of the prequel trilogy.

The first trilogy (well, maybe not *Return)* was created by grownups who remembered what it was like to be a child, for an audience of adults who remembered what it was like to be a child. It spoke directly to our remember of the sense of wonder we felt when reading those books, comics, watching those serials.

It seemed as though the prequel trilogy was created by grownups who had started to forget what it was like to be a child, for an audience of children. Or rather, an audience of what they thought children are like. Except they themselves had forgotten.

Phantom Menace, with its midichlorians, its wooden acting and with the misbegotten Jar Jar Binks, was in some ways grimace-worthy. But it had redemptive moments. The *Ben-Hur* like "chariot race" was so much fun that one did feel like a child again. The costumes and effects were so grand and so gorgeous that they pretty much overwhelmed what thin story there was, but they were still great. I have to admit that I only saw it in the theater a couple of times.

The next two films really did feel to me like one long film. It's blasphemy, I know, but I didn't even see the third one in the theater. The journey the characters take is already known, so what could have made the films more watchable would have been character development, aided by decent, intense acting. Hayden Christiansen was good looking. But to mutate credibly from the likeable Jake to the most hated monster in the galaxy is a task for a master actor.

If midichlorians and Jar Jar were the blight of *Phantom*, the dreary politics were the bane of the whole trilogy. In science fiction, there can be a lot of politics — people exerting control over planets, backstabbing, devising clever plots — but the politics of the prequel trilogy is just ... not inventive enough to play out against a galactic backdrop. Machiavellian planet-grabbings abound in SF novels and can be enthralling. Here they are about as interesting as a school board meeting.

The next two films led me very far from the childlike sense of wonder, into a labyrinth of stunning imagery and silly names, into attempt after attempt to chronicle Anakin's journey into the heart of darkness. He was certainly scripted into doing things that would have been unheard of in the first trilogy — like performing the Jedi equivalent of a school shooting. But somehow, it was a bit too cartooony to feel evil. The council of Jedi masters resembled a geriatric edition of the original 1960s Legion of Superheroes. And Count Dooku, aka Dracula? Gimme a break.

It boiled down to a conflict between two contradictory lines of evolution. On the one hand, the prequels wanted to look at more grownup themes — mass murder, politics and "science". On the other, as I've mentioned, they were also trying to cash in on the toys in a big way and conscious of the youth of the audience in a way that was not true of the original series (until *Return.)*

This contradiction showed up most clearly in the prequels' handling of war. Death was used sparingly in the original trilogy — well, Alderan, but when one blows up a planet, that's all very well but we're not identifying with any characters — but here were talking wars with vast numbers of entities presumably having to be bumped off. Solving this ethical problem of having children's movies with lots of people dying was through the liberal use of mechanical armies — rows and rows and rows of burly droids and clanking machines — which could be chopped up, sliced, diced and discarded without bloodshed.

The inner child is not easily deceived. And real children usually know when they're being talked down to. So this was an uneasy balancing act for both audiences. And yet....

It turned out that we adults with our jealously guarded inner child, our self-important blandishments about our sense of wonder ... we were wrong about one thing. We might have seen through some of the crasser elements of this — but kids *did* go for it. It *did* speak to them. A whole new gang joined the club in droves. *Star Wars* became a multi-gen phenomenon. That would be the very best reason for waiting so long — our kids had grown up and now both we *and* our children could bond over something we loved.

Soon there would be a bunch of characters who, while not endowed with the ability to wisecrack in the face of certain death as in the first trilogy, would be the coolest ever action figures. Did we really care about Darth Maul's character arc? No, but he looked cool. And when he flashed that double saber to the quasi-religious choral epic invocation (composed by John Williams using a Sanskrit text) who could not feel a thrill? A thrill relived each time you took the action figure out of the box?

I really think that in the end it was the toys that saved the prequel trilogy.

Then came another trilogy ... or in a sense, a pentalogy, with two more movies tendrilling into the joints between trilogies. The two side movies were about as contrasting as you could get: *Rogue One,* in which one knew from the nature of the plot that none of the protagonists would survive it, had a hard-edged inexorability and an uncompromising quality that was very attractive to the people like me, who had had to take the prequel trilogy with a grain of salt. For me the greatest experience of all was to see Peter Cushing being resurrected through the miracle of twenty-first century film technology.

Solo, on the other hand was pure compromise. It almost seemed to have been made by Disney. Which, of course, it was. Nevertheless, it was a perfectly acceptable swashbuckler and should be enjoyed as just that. It wasn't bad, just *bleh.* I admit that I enjoyed it tremendously, though that is not a popular opinion. On the other hand, I watched it on Netflix.

The sequel trilogy was the thing on which the whole thing hung. Another generation, almost, had gone by. We had had decades of nitpicking — purists fighting against Lucas's endless penchant for reconforming the video, softening Han's personality, enlarging Tatooine and filling it with CGI, dumping an alien CGI Jabba the Hutt into the first film and so on. (Before he appeared in *Return of the Jedi,* Jabba had not been imagined as a gigantic jelly on springs.) Fans had plenty of controversy, but with the new trilogy, controversy reigned supreme.

Let's start with the concept of *mirroring*.   There
seems to have been a clear desire to have the prequel
trilogy run in a parallel structure to the original.   And
this "rhyming" can be seen very clearly.   There are
actually *shot for shot* echoes that thematically tie the
two trilogies today, suggesting a more sophisticated
overview that might be thought.

Thus, fans believed that mirroring would occur in
the third trilogy as well and there was definitely reason
to start noticing it in *The Force Awakens*.   Even the
poster, which was obviously inspired by the original, fed
into this idea.   And so yes, we have a younger crowd of
rebellious misfits — and a very Luke Skywalker-ish
female character — a heroine with mysterious origins
wearing a not dissimilar outfit — a rakish pilot — a
desert and so on.   Plus the *fansābisu* appearances of the
old guard — while the audience in Thailand didn't
applaud when I saw the film (at an unadvertised
preview a day before even most Americans)   I can
imagine the audience at the Uptown clapping wildly
each time a venerable figure from the past emerged.

Would the *Force Awakens* also awaken our childlike
sense of wonder?   We were all hoping against hope —
like a dumped lover who can't let go.   And J.J. Abrams is
a master of nostalgia, so yes, every button was pushed,
and then some.   Sure, it was manipulative but we all
loved it.   Unremarked on were the midichlorians, and
politics was rarely mentioned.   Echoing the
generationalism of the three trilogies, this trilogy
featured offspring — Kylo Ren mainly — torn between
darkness and light.   There's a super-weapon.   It was in
effect a re-imagining of the first film, grittier than the
CGI-laden prequel trilogy, with cameos by everyone we
had loved in the 1977.   What was there to not like about
The Force Awakens?

Well — Snoke didn't have the gleeful drama-queen villainousness of the Emperor. Kylo didn't have the sheer charisma of Darth Vader as a villain. However, he made up for that in complexity. In a few short scenes, Kylo Ren managed to go through all the emotional depth and inner conflict that young Anakin had not managed in interminable sequences. And though we loved Han, we all secretly hoped that would be no last minute softening of Kylo's will — because inner darkness needed to be *real* for the film to work.

Now, Leia was a strong woman character in the first film. Now she's a general, so her strength clearly continues. Yet she's also a woman of the 1970s — she gets rescued, wears a skimpy sex-slave costume in *Return* — whereas Rey is a woman of the twenty-teens — she can everything a man can do — more efficiently and without breaking a sweat. Everyone fell in love with Rey and praised the film's political correctness, as well.

All of us sexagenarians felt a surge of returned youth. And couldn't wait for *The Last Jedi*.

Which turned out to be the most controversial — and misunderstood — of all the films. It deflected expectations, seemed to ignore canon, made us hate our heroes. But I would argue that it is one of the more interesting films in the sequence precisely because it doesn't do anything we expect.

Everyone found something to dislike in *The Last Jedi*, so perhaps I should take about some of its positives. At the heart of this film, which, like *Empire* and *Attack*, has as its main driving force the training of a young apprentice — whether towards the light or the dark — there is a cave of mirrors, and Rey must come face to face with herself. With this scene as anchor, we realize that the mirror structure of the three trilogies is intact.

There are nuances in Rey's relationship with Kylo Ren that genuinely cause us to have ambiguous feelings. As for Luke's story arc — don't get the average fan talking, you'll get an earful! Mark Hamill himself was rumored to be wildly bitching about it.

And everyone has superpowers not even hinted at in previous films. The final confrontation with essentially a "virtual" Luke battling the entire forces of evil is a quantitative *and* qualitative leap in "superpower index" — much like the end of David Lynch's *Dune* where the annoying little girl dumps the ocean of one planet into another planet through the sheer force of her mind.

The sense of having lost our moorings, that *anything* can happen that can upset the entire applecart of the Lucasverse, is actually the strongest feature of this film and I'm not upset that the penultimate movie should be one that deliberately stirs up strong feelings. And yeah, it is heresy, but I kind of liked it.

This dichotomy made the radical course correction of *Skywalker* both disappointing and welcomed as the inevitable, logical, and fitting conclusion of the epic. *Fansābisu* was deployed in so many permutations that that question was never *who* would appear next, but *how* they were going to shoehorn it in. It's only been three days since I've seen this thing but I have to say that I found the first few minutes a little soporific, waking up with a start to the sight of the slightly queaseworthy resurrection of General Leia.

Bleating and cackling, Palpatine soon put paid to the spectre of the spineless Snoke. In its haste to reverse engineer all of *The Last Jedi's* false leads, exposition was breathless. If you blinked, you missed how Palpatine had really been manipulating *everything* all the time from the beginning. A few seconds of retconning and the whole ennealogy set to rights!

And as many loose ends as possible tied up, the expository lumps sticking out like undissolved nodules of instant coffee. We were worried about unstated incestuous subtexts between Leia and Luke? Rey and Ren are free to kiss, though by the unwritten rules of boy's adventure stories, one of the pair must immediately drop dead — well, dematerialize and become one with the Force — so the other can remain a Lone Warrior. In the now expected unexpected twist, it's the girl who goes on living.

The big bad battle scene at the end has more destroyers, x-wings, tie fighters and random space vehicles that one can imagine sharing a single screen. Boy, is it epic! Yeah, and there's even a long *Lord of the Rings* style "envoi" as we say farewell to all the survivors and see what will become of them. Mercifully it's a much shorter coda than the one in *Rings*.

Loose end I most wish was tied? The little boy with the broom at the end of *Last Jedi*. I was imagining a whole big adventure for him. And least? I really do not want to know how Anakin's immaculate conception was achieved, and couldn't care less about the Whills.

I could have said a lot more about something that has, after all, consumed more than four decades of my life on earth. We're living in a kind of cornucopia of Warsie product now. I haven't watched *Mandalorian* — forgot to pay my VPN bill — and I catch the animated episodes on plane journeys from time to time. This deluge is not going to slow down.

And yet —

Was there ever a moment as thrillingly doom-laden as "That's no moon!" Was there ever a villain so self-confidently misguided as Peter Cushing grating out the line "Evacuate? In our moment of triuph? I think you oveRRRestimate their chances!"? We've had a lot of "bad feelings about this" — but were any of them quite as disturbing as the first time? And was there ever a comeback like "I love you!" — "I know." —? Did anyone ever answer the question "Who's your daddy?" more terrifyingly than Darth Vader?

I find your lack of faith disturbing.

The memory of the Uptown is as vivid now as it was then. The excitement. The collective, quasi-religious awe generated in our army of the nerdy. The moment lives for ever. After forty-two years, one truth remains: *The Force will be with you always.*

The Web Dancer was the second of the stories I published set in the *Inquestor* world. It doesn't have characters in common with *The Thirteenth Utopia* and has a different feel to it, and it's the first one to deal with childhood which becomes one of the series' prevalent themes — even though some characters are hundreds if not thousands of years old.

Lost Tales
The Web Dancer

She was poised in the pause on a leap's edge, toes nudging the rope-slack in the tight circlet of glare, pressed between a breath and its release—a girl of eleven, alone under a billion unseen eyes.

This time—

Nika flexed her toes swiftly for the first triple somersault of her career. She gathered in all the strands of tension and compressed them, *hard*, into a knot of neutronium deep within herself, then released it all at once, exploded outward at the ends of her limbs, *gave* into the perfect curve of the movement-

And slipped!

There was a moment between falling and fallen. A moment drawn out and still. A moment of cutting clarity. In that moment her gray eyes saw—

—image boxes slamming to the ground, lens-jewels splintering, fire cartwheeling over instrument banks, doorways dominoing over monitors and shelfstands, and—

(It wasn't my fault I slipped! she thought. *Something collided with the show satellite! There's a war going on in this system and we should never have chosen to record here but they said we were neutral and paJonners can't be touched because they come under the protection if the Inquest!)*

—technicians were running amok, alien uniforms of different sides flashed across the floor, bodies cascaded like flocks of birds, someone in a booming voice declaring this quadrant of space now occupied, performers with mouths open staring at the slaughter, screaming

(She closed her eyes then. *I'm going to die!* she thought, not caring anymore. *I'm just going to be a chance victim ifsomeone else's war...*and then she wished her hair was streaming above her, not cropped to a centimeter's length, but then she remembered why she had cut it off, and she felt a yawning emptiness inside her and wanted to die.)

—rope flopping snakelike, writhing, tangling her feet, and*(I don't care!* she thought fiercely. *I'm Nika ifthe clan ifRax and the show never stops, never never never-)*

The vault of the show satellite cracked. Through the airshield the stars shone...and another ship, huge, with none of the gaudy local markings, was growing rapidly, blacking out the starlight.

Who could they be? she wondered, in the split second before the forceshield slapped her into blackness.

Nika opened her eyes. *(Why am I still alive?* she thought.) "They're all dead." The voice was gravelly, the accent strange. "Don't think of them anymore. Be at peace with yourself."

Silhouettes of two men; and behind them...She could not tell where the room ended and where the wild dance of laser-bright lights began. Flametongues whipped against blackness! And darting between them, neckerchief swirls of purple, crimson, cerulean, cadmium-yellow, ultramarine, bursting out and fading into darkness .

...~'re *in a starship!* For they were in the overcosm then: that *other* space, of strange dimensions, where *jar* becomes *near.*

"Dead?" She faced her captors. *How much time had passed?* She could still feel the tightrope slipping from her feet and the utter helplessness...

"Dead," the gravelly voice echoed. "We won't harm you, girl. We saved your life."

He was good looking, bland, overdressed; his body-jewels gleamed in the rainbow fire of outside. She disliked him at once. The other one, though: severe, old, dressed from head to foot in a single shimmercloak.

An Inquestor! So somehow, power was involved. A lot of power.

It wasn't the first time Nika had been whisked away from everything she knew. *I'm so tired,* she thought... she wanted to cry. But she knew she would not. She had vowed never to cry again.

"They are all dead, your friends," said the Inquestor, not unkindly. "Some might have survived a month or two...but time dilation has taken care of *them.* We intercepted a local battle to pluck you out."

"But the Inquest doesn't interfere in local wars!" she said. When that evoked no response, she cried out, "I could have *done* it!"

"Done what?" said the first man.

"The triple somersault!" she said. "The climax of my career, recorded on crystals for a billion eyes."

"Career!" the young man scoffed. "Don't mock her," said the Inquestor sharply. "Kaz Amar, go back to your astrogating." The man bowed, departed quickly. "You're a child yet," the Inquestor said when they were alone. "Let's not hear talk of crowning moments of careers, Nika, not for another century yet."

Nika felt rage gathering inside her. *I'm not a child!* How dare they patronize her! They had taken away everything: her homeworld, her friends, the nomadic life of the show-satellites, flicking from system to system...and they had plucked her away from her supreme achievement.

(She felt the rope slipping beneath her feet again. She would have struck out in fury —)

Then she heard inside herself the voice of Iliash, who had trained her: *Push your rage inward! Let it collapse like the aftermath ofa nova, into a ball of neutronium! Harder, harder...*the voice pounded at her memory...

"Nikkyeh—" the other began, consolingly. *"Nika.* I'm not a child." How dare he presume to address her by a diminutive, when he was neither lover nor friend.

"Good, you have personal dignity, spirit," said the Inquestor, appraising her.

"Take me *home!"*

The Inquestor stood impassive. He towered over her, a darkened doorway set into the wall of light-swirls. "Nika—"

"I won't stay here! I have to get back to homeworld. If I train hard I can make the panhuman games. You don't have the right to kidnap me." But she felt her past slipping away, she saw that she no longer believed in homeworld or in herself...

"Nika," said the Inquestor. "You are a Rax, and we have need of a Rax. You've grown up thinking you're nothing special, just fit for the circus; your body too small for a warrior, your intellect too unschooled for a thinker. But you are one of the most valuable people in the Dispersal of Man. You're not ready for all this yet. You should have had more time, more training. But we're desperate."

"For what?"

"Listen. I am Ton Exkandar z Vangyvel K'Ning, Inquestor and Kingling."

"Ruler of my homeworld..." Blurred images of infancy whirlpooled.

"Yes. Don't say I didn't have the right to kidnap you." He paused. Behind, fireworks burst from a sea of ink. Fire-ripples laced the darkness. *Why is he trying to justify himself?* Nika thought. Then: *He's vulnerable.* She wanted to trust him, but —

"It is incredible that we should need you!" he burst out. "That I should gatecrash a petty war, like a space pirate, a common kidnapper—"

"But why do you need me?" She was bewildered, angry, frightened. "Did you destroy the show-satellite just to get *me?*"

"No," said Ton Exkandar, "we intercepted the local war. You *had* to be saved." *Am I that important? I'm only a girl! What sort of game am I a pawn in?*

"And now I'll never do it..."

"Do what?"

But Nika had shut him out of her thoughts. She had turned away from him; and now she watched the shifting, soundless patterns, letting them soothe her, hypnotize her...

She imagined an infinite rope stretched all the way across the overcosm, and infinite Nikas, reflections of herself, leaping, upending themselves in a swift tight arc of movement, whirling down to touch the rope with the gentlest of touches...

And slipping. It was closed-loop holotape of the memory, each time no less terrifying.

How could she fight these people? She didn't know who they were and what they wanted. And she had fought too many people already to become what she was. She was tired! Drained!

"And now I'll never do it," she said, shuddering.

She would not let them put her into stasis. So there would be three subjective months in the overcosm, and there was nothing to do.

In her quarters there was one curved gray wall which could be blanked and which gave a view of the madness outside. When she was awake she lay on her pallet and watched.

They had put up a series of ranked transverse bars for her to practice on. But she wouldn't touch them. She didn't even look at them. Because they made her suspect her whole childhood had been manipulated, had been drawn toward...something no one would tell her about.

There was nothing to do but remember. And this she did, in the moments before sleep, or after staring herself into a trance while the colors danced...

She was six and the children had all gone to war. She had run all the way from the orphanage to watch them, to stand by the wall and see the ships rise like a flock of silverdoves and cross the faces of the far, cold suns of Vangyvel.

Mother found her weeping under a whispertree. It reached out a furcoated metal hand to the child's brow; and the tree sang as the breezes of Vangyvel touched its flutelike leaves, a soft random counterpoint..."Don't cry," said Mother in its consoling mode.

"I want to go, too!"

"So you shall, so you shall...but right now you're too small. Too precious, too special," it said, increasing its sympathy-tones in a steep gradient with each word.

"There's something wrong with me! I know it, I know it!" She began sobbing again, with the utter, end-of-the-universe hopelessness that only children know. For a while now she had not grown at all, and her bones were thin and hollow. "I'm a mutant or something! Isn't that why I'm in an orphanage?"

"Of course not, child, you're very special, only I can't tell you why yet..."

And the froglet will become a Kingling! thought Nika, bitter. Mother was programmed to lie to her. After all, it was only a machine. The tree seemed to copy her sobs, mocking them, the way the other children always did...

"I'll never cry again!" she said passionately. "I'll do something with my tiny body that no one else will be able to do!"

"That's my girl."

"All right, Mother. Nikkyeh will go home now." They stepped toward the displacement plate and commanded the coordinates. That was the day she had first felt the emptiness inside, yearning to be filled. And had thrown anger into it.

Later she threw herself into dancing the rope. She had to be good at *something!* And she was. Her sense of balance was *unnatural,* everyone said. Which was true.

She could spin like a gyroscope down half the length of a slackrope. She could do it slowly, making them blue from holding their collective breath, stretch out the tension to its elastic limits, then reverse in a flash, stifling the gasps of relief.

Rax Iliash was her teacher. They brought him in, encouraging her. He was older, about twelve or so, she judged, but small, too, like her. Two years he spent pushing her. He knew so much, he who seemed just a child.

The moments when she released all her anger at being different, all her frustration at not being normal, perhaps—into achingly beautiful parabolas of motion across emptiness—these were her moments of joy. Finally they made crystals of her dancing, and they became nomads. The homeless life of the show-satellites pleased Nika—what had home meant but children's mocking laughter?

On initiation, she, too, had received the clan title of Rax. She and Iliash were the only two either of them had ever heard of. She never took part in the initiation; the Inquestor of Judgment had merely handed the title to her..."But am I not to be tested?" She was suspicious as always, of everyone except Iliash.

Worried, overworked, the eyes had looked right through her and he said: "Daughter, you are Rax. We cannot waste you." *What did that mean?*

Once she and Iliash had gone to the zoo world and wandered around like tourists, gaping at the pseudo-environments: the firesnows of Ont, the methane fogs of Brekekekex, the rivermountains of Ellory, the amber skies of Lalaparalla; and the beasts: lobster-things, fire-things, cloud-things, balloon-things...

Two innocents, they walked hand in hand. Between the forceshielded habitats were corridors of a manworld environment. They came to a cave where a crystal creature slept. The crowd lurched forward as it woke.

Suddenly a burst of anguish issued from the cave and hit Nika, almost physically. "Did you *feel* that?"

"Yes. Yes." His gray eyes, so like hers, were troubled. The crowd was unaware of anything; they bent down, almost touching the force shield, murmuring, "Oh, how cute..."

Iliash's hands almost squashed Nika's. Waves of pain crested and ebbed. "I can't stand it!" she said. Then, crying out "It's a mistake! That's a sentient creature! You can't cage him!"

Curious stares, laughter. She was being mocked again! She was almost fainting with the pain. Iliash pulled her and dragged her along the path, away from the crowd.

Now they reached a field, with ten-meter-high cornstalks under an ink-blue sky. Iliash was saying, "Nikkyeh, you and I have this empathy. It's one of our special things, an empathy with alien beings. You and I are *tailored*, Nikkyeh! The Inquest has some purpose for us."

She clutched him to her. But they were just two children, and nothing came of it.

Soon after the show-satellite left for another system, Nika began to train for the triple somersault in 0.5 gravity. No rope dancer had ever done it before. She worked with a fierceness not usually found in children. She had to fill the void inside her! She was hungry for training...

And so she forgot all about the Inquest's special purpose. It seemed so irrelevant. She was far from Vangyvel now; and the Dispersal of Man comprised a respectable percentage of the galaxy.

But when she was nine Iliash left the troupe.

She went to say goodbye to him. They were on a desert planet, a dreary planet of endless red sand under a sapphire sky. Iliash stood...strange how he had never grown at all...beside two tall figures in shimmercloaks. Inquestors! And behind the three-

It was a sphere. It was totally black, featureless, perhaps ten meters in diameter. It appeared to have no substance. It was as if a portion of the sandscape and sky had been blotted out, had simply ceased to exist. It was a tachyon bubble, of course. Inquestors used them to travel instantly through space. Never ordinary people. The overcosm still required subjective time of the traveler, even though it was, in effect, faster than light. The overcosm had its own overcosm, and it was through these highest planes that the tachyon devices traveled, short-cutting the short-cuts.

It was black because it was not even part of the universe. And only the Inquest could use them, because of the devastating energy waste, and because it might lend too much power to the lower clans.

Nika was afraid. *Two* Inquestors! A tachyon bubble! So Iliash had to be important, somehow.

But he was just a kid!

She looked at the boy whose gray eyes so resembled her own, who shared her clan name, whom she was about to lose forever. Would they come for her, too?

"You're all I have, Ilyeh!"

The two Inquestors moved impatiently. There was not much time. "Ilyeh." She held his hand tight. "Nikkyeh," he said, "I've learned what the Inquest made us for.

Now I'm going away to do what I have to do..."

She raged impotently. *Push it inside yourself, the neutronium ball!* "I love you, Ilyeh," she said. (*Do I?* she asked herself.) "When we're older, if time dilation hasn't made us too far apart in age—"

"Don't talk about what can't be!" he said. His eyes looked wistful, yet hopeless.

"What do you mean?"

"You and I—" He stopped suddenly, turning to see whether they were watching him. "We don't have puberty. We don't grow. How old am I, Nikkyeh? How old do you think? I'm *eighty-seven!*" Nika chose to ignore this; she could not believe it. "You can refuse to go," she pleaded. "They made us too well," said Ihash. "They made us so we'll *want* to do this, they put the love of it in our bones..."

"Of *what?*" she said sullenly. "There's nothing I love more than you!"

"There is, there is!" He turned to go. The two Inquestors had faded into the tachyon bubble, and one of his feet had already vanished into the blob. She felt abandoned, lied to. He was like Mother after all.

"What do you mean?" she shouted. "What is there that I love more than you?"

"That triple somersault!" he said. He blew her a kiss, wrenched himself around and leaped into the bubble. It winked out. There was no trace of it on the sand, only three sets of footprints that led to the same spot and vanished...she turned away and began to walk toward the landing craft.

Now she felt truly empty. Even Iliash, whom she had trusted, had finally betrayed her. *The triple somersault!* The cruelty of it! How could he make fun of her like this?

But it was true.

That was the day she cut off all her hair, disgusted with herself. And determined to think of nothing at all but the triple somersault, to feed all her anger to the triple somersault!

"Why don't you use the bars?" Exkandar asked, gently. It had been two months; and—abandoning her past in despair-Nika had grown her hair again. It was long now, and fiery as a bursting star.

"When the birds aren't happy, they don't sing."

"As you wish."

"Why do they all treat me so condescendingly here?" she said, sounding suddenly frail. Exkandar said: "You're indispensable; they're not. They're afraid of you, really."

"But why?"

"You'll see."

She watched one swirl of green flame as it slowly transformed into a crazy spiral and melded into the blackness. *"You'll see! You'll see!* Do you people never tell anyone anything?"

"Nika, I don't know that you could take it yet. You're too young. I counseled against all this—"

"Well, give me a clue!"

"All right," he said heavily. "We need more starships. There is to be a war, a war with aliens..."

"That has nothing to do with me. Performers are neutral."

"Wait, listen to me!" *How tired he sounds!* Nika thought. "How do starships work? You should know that."

Nika laughed. "They're navigated through the overcosm," she said, "by an astrogator who is in communion with a delphinoid shipmind—" When Exkandar did not answer, she went on, "Delphinoids are giant creatures who are all brain. They're captured on... some planet, I don't know. They perceive the overcosm directly. They're cybernetically implanted into ships by means of...some crystal or other..."

"Yes," said Exkandar. "There are semi sentient crystals that can concentrate and focus particle streams into the overcosm."

"But," Nika said, "they never told us, in school, where the crystals come from."

"And there is your clue," said Exkandar, and would say no more.

Nika thought it over. She had been tailored-gene-tailored-for empathy with alien minds, for minimal physical development. They needed starships. The ships needed crystals. *It doesn't make any sense!*

Exkandar said, "I want you to keep practicing. Use the bars, Nika." She saw them, light finger-thin poles of some flexible polymer, stretched from wall to wall in ranks of increasing height. For a moment only she wanted to rush up to them and spring into action, leaping from one to the other till she could dance on the highest pole...

"No," she said. *Am I punishing them or myself?* Exkandar took this as a dismissal and left. And Nika wondered at this, that her word could command a Kingling and Inquestor.

Then, making sure she was unobserved, she flashed up in an easy bound onto the first rung, then from one ranked bar to the next as though they were steps in a pyramid. When she reached the highest one, she tiptoed swiftly along the bar, her weight hardly flexing it at all. Her mind wandered...

She caught her balance. *Out of practice!* She remembered how she had fallen, and then the bar slithered from under her; quickly she grabbed with her hands and pulled herself up again...

Oh, no. They've winded me. There was a new kind of queasiness in her stomach. *I'm afraid!* she thought, startled by the new emotion.

In a few days they reached a nameless planet that intersected a nexus in the tachyon universe. It was a blizzard-swept place, without inhabitants save for the nexus station crew, all of the clan of Nartak, another one Nika had never encountered.

The two of them came down in a lander to await their tachyon bubble. High overhead, it materialized, blotting out more and more of the snowburst as it descended, sinking through the domeroof as though it were thin air. There was a humming; another Inquestor, also in a plain shimmercloak, emerged from the black blot.

Disappointment showed on the stranger's face. "Only one?"

"We could trace no others," said Exkandar quickly. "And this is a youngling of eleven."

"It's a catastrophe!" said the visitor. "Come, both of you." To Exkandar: "Is she prepared?" He toyed with his shimmercloak.

"She doesn't know anything," said Exkandar. "The circumstances of her presence with us were...traumatic; I thought it best—"

"Yes, yes." He blotted out. Exkandar pushed the girl ahead into the bubble; once inside she could not tell she was *inside* at all. They moved, suddenly, into the air, and Nika felt no excitement or wonder, only the same deadness she had felt since her capture. But just before they blinked out-

This is where they took Iliash!

She closed her eyes and remembered his face, as though she were looking into a mirror: the eyes that reflected her own, the boyishness that, she now knew, concealed long experience.

She smiled...for the first time since the attack on the satellite...and clutched the memory of his face to her, determined never to let it slip.

Bleak. Gray. Bleak. Gray.

It was an impossibly tiny planet, with a horizon that dropped too soon, like an asteroid's: its diameter was only fifty kilometers. There was a core of neutronium, the size of a wine-goblet perhaps, denser even than the degenerate matter of white dwarfs, they said. Or perhaps a seething soup of quarks, or perhaps compressed all the way into a black hole...whatever it was, it gave the planet a surface gravity of 0.78.

She hated the planet!

It had crazy naked crags, gray and featureless, that erupted out of gray, mirror-still lakes. The sky was gray, too, an even, impenetrable gray like Iliash's eyes, like Nika's eyes.

Nika and Exkandar hovered in the floater over the mountains. "It's artificial, this planet," she said. It was obvious. But instead of wondering at it, she detested it.

"Yes," said Exkandar, "but not built by us. Not by humans. By a race long extinct. A world built to order, built for the breeding of the tam crystals. We haven't worked out every variable. We can't duplicate what this world does! The neutronium core, for instance-we don't know how vital that is. If it is, we can't replicate it at all."

The floater swooped toward the frighteningly close horizon, whipping aside to avoid the crag. Nika heard a quiet rumbling, almost beneath the threshold of hearing. "What's that sound?" she asked. And felt herself *drawn* to the sound somehow, attracted by it.

"The mountains are in heat."

"Oh." The two days she had spent here had only compounded her bewilderment. Something brushed her face. She started to strike out at it in annoyance...

She looked up to see a monstrous butterfly, with a wingspan of perhaps a meter, hovering ahead. She let out a little scream, more in surprise than fright.

The animal hovered. The resemblance to a butterfly was only superficial, she saw. It had uncountable tiers of wings, each paper-thin and translucent, refracting light into a thousand colors. There were two legs, crystalline and muscular at the same time...and a small, oval head with six or seven eyelike organs. From the head sprouted paper fans—they looked like fans—that glittered intermittently as they caught the light...the wings moved, vibrated faster than the eye could see; and then were suddenly still as a wind sprang up to support the creature. The fans rotated nervously, catching at sunlight; there was little of it here, for the sun was perpetually hidden in veils of gray cloud.

The creature watched the floater and its occupants for a long time. They were buoyed up by the same air current.

Angel, thought Nika, *faery, creature of myth*...her heart almost stopped beating. Something in the void inside her responded to it...

Suddenly the creature shivered all over, spread its wings, vibrated them, a shimmering aurora of lights splashed across the grayness, a whir of wings, a dazzling soaring into the cloudbanks that left an after image like the ghost of a rainbow...

So beautiful! "If only I were like it," she said, "and not trapped the way I am."

"It is a farfal," said Exkandar. "The farfellor are the larval forms..."

"Of what?" she said as they rounded another precipice and skimmed a lake of deathly stillness.

"Of the tarn creatures."

"There are beasts, then, living in the mountains?" She tried not to sound too interested, but in spite of herself..."No. They *are* the mountains." Nika whipped around in panic, upsetting the floater for a moment. She saw the torturous crags, straddling the horizon, twisted shapes that strained toward the ash-gray cloudveils...

"Whoever built this planet was far superior to us, in technology, in bioengineering...tam crystals, the things that focus the minds of delphinoid ships, are the unfertilized ova of these mountains," said Exkandar. "The adult forms are static, vast, siliconbased; photosynthesizing silicon chains from the gray sunlight and from the silicate-rich crust, the salts dissolved in the lakewater. Perhaps their roots even reach down to the neutronium core—there are unsolved anomalies in its particle emissions—and draw on its energy. We don't know exactly how it works, just that it's a very lucky thing for the Dispersal of Man, a secret stumbled on many millennia ago which has kept the human race in contact with itself, which has stabilized and enriched our culture..."

So that's how the Inquest keeps control oj the Dispersal oj Man, thought Nika. *And it's such a precarious secret, too. They're so* vulnerable. *Without the crystals, war and commerce would both cease.*

But what does it have to do with me?

"The clan of Rax...we are collectors of tam crystals, then?" she said. *It's humiliating!* she thought. *To scrabble in the rocks, when I could have been the Dispersal's greatest rope dancer.* It didn't sound possible.

"Let's float onward." He blinked, and Nika knew that he was keying the floater by means of a brain-implant. Soon they soared above the lake and swerved around a peak, with the horizon gaining on them...

They reached a plateau encircled by a wall of stubbier mountains. A flock of farfellor swooped by the mountain-face and swung upward, in a perfect arc, like a necklace drawn up by an unseen hand.

The floater came to rest near the edge of the plateau and they stepped down. The rumbling came again. "Is that what you meant, when you said the mountain was *in heat?*"

"They have cycles. Now look ahead of you." Nika obeyed him. For a moment she had forgotten she was a prisoner, destined for an unknown and probably unpleasant fate.

Gray statues of farfellor stood on the plateau's edge, staring out over the emptiness at the ring of tam creatures. Nika went up and touched one, tentatively; its touch was cold as marble. Now two or three farfellor, circling overhead, swooped down in a wild glittering and landed beside them, and stopped moving. As she watched, veins of grayness grew and spread across the color-lattice of wings, across the crystalline legs

"They're dying!" she gasped.

"No, metamorphosing...in a few years, a century perhaps, another tam creature will grow here. There is an active phase of reproduction. After that the mountain is quiet, and never moves again; it might be dead or dormant, we don't know. Are they sentient, Nika? You were bred for empathy with aliens..."

She listened for the cries of other minds. But she could not tell. There could have been a voice, but it was a murmur so distant that it might have come from another world. "I don't know."

"None of you ever know, for sure."

What an alien world! And she was so alone in it. She pushed ever harder at her fear, hoping it would contract to nothing. "But where are the other Rax? Where is Iliash?" She knew he was withholding something. "Why us? Do we have to die to get your precious crystals out of the mountains, is that it?" For a moment Nika longed for the touch of Mother's fur-covered iron hand...*but I mustn't be a child!* she thought. *Must fight...*

"It's hard for me to tell you, little one. We Inquestors," Exkandar paused, choosing his words, "are above all compassionate; at initiation we are selected for this trait. I can't bring myself to—"

What could it be that upset him so? Nika could imagine only death. Panic pounded at her. She sprang up and bolted for the floater. When she reached it he had already caught her.

"No, it's not what you think!" he shouted. "Come, let me finish what I have to show you." And again he seemed so vulnerable that Nika felt for him; though she knew that she was the victim, not he.

Some forty kilometers on there was a peak, especially huge, going right up through the clouds. They flew into a small building, open on three sides, built into the foot of the mountain; steps were carved into it, and there were other houses, a small village. Peopleguards or workmen—in blinding bright tunics, were milling around the hallway. When they saw Exkandar they bowed; when they saw Nika they gaped.

At the end of the hall there was a tiny passageway, circular, maybe a meter wide. It led to total darkness.

It's a tunnel! she thought. *They're going to force me in there and make me dig around for the eggs....*"You can't make me go in there!" she said, hysterically. "The other Rax are lost in the tunnels, aren't they? You bred us small to make us live out our lives in there? I won't do it! I'm a rope dancer, I need the open—"

Exkandar stared at her incredulously, then burst out laughing, for the first time since she'd known him. One of the workers said quickly: "Lord Inquestor, she doesn't know?" The mountain rumbled a little. The workers fell on their knees and seemed to be deep in prayer.

"They don't know the truth," Exkandar whispered to Nika. "They worship the tam creatures. They're the egg-collectors, they gather them as they roll down the oviducts—that's what the tunnels are—and they'll worship you, too! We've set it up as a religion to conceal what the eggs really are..."

"Then what *is* my role?" Nika was exasperated beyond endurance. "What happened to Iliash? Didn't you bring a Rax named Iliash here?"

Exkandar took her by the hand. "I'll show you now."

At the entrance they boarded the floater and wafted upward, following the gradient of the tam, hugging the surface. Nika strained to see some crack, some irregularity of color or texture. There was none; it was all one gray.

They glided onto a perch of the cliff-face. The Inquestor jumped off and motioned her to look. At first she saw nothing-

Then-

Growing out of the cliff edge, flung out taut over the chasm till it disappeared into the grayness, was a tightrope. Nika ran to the edge, got down on her knees and leaned over to touch it. It felt...made for her. The slackness of it was just right, the pressure just enough. A stadium out in the wilderness, on an unnamed planet!

Something inside her responded at last. She yearned to walk the strand...

Her eye ran along the rope, and she saw faint lines alongside it, crossing over it, above and below...mostly, the lines were invisible, until the light fell just right, until the wind tugged gently on them.

She put one foot forward, and remembered

(Rope slipping from under her, wild vertigo of burning machinery and people aflame, *whirling—I've been kidnapped! I should be angry! I shouldn't do anything they want me to do!*)

And fear. The fear that had come to her for the first time, unbidden, when she had tried to practice again on the ship. She tried to swallow it up, kneeling down and caressing the rope, pulling at the tension...

Exkandar explained. 'These strands are the tam creature's nervous system. When it is in heat, the larval forms...and you...will feel it calling you; the farfellor fly over and dance lightly on the strands, stimulating the sleeping mountain...after a while, sometimes half an hour, sometimes half a day or more, the eggs are released, one by one, sliding down the tunnels to the oviductmouths. The dancing farfal sends out empathy-signals all over the planet, and thousands of farfellor flock to the tunnel mouth to fertilize the eggs, making tempests with their wings, breaking the sides of the mountain in their urgency...

"And after, they are too exhausted. They have spent everything; their fertilizing fluid, their reserves of energy-for farfellor do not ingest—and with their last strength they fly to a plateau, become rooted and dormant, await the next stage of their cycle. Thousands of them will eventually merge into a single mountain—"

And suddenly, Nika saw what he was driving at. "I have to dance on the webstrands!" she cried out. And it came to her at once, how she had been manipulated at every stage in her life.

"Don't blame us, Nika!" Exkandar said, anguished. "If there were another way we would have found it. But we need *unfertilized* ova! And if the dancer does not send out signals to the other farfellor, the eggs are not fertilized. We tried using robots and androids and altered animals...but nothing works except a human being, reacting to impulses given off by the alien mind, small, perfectly in control of his body—"

"Can't you slaughter them as they attack the mountain? Can't you set up forceshields?"

"The mountain senses if there are any obstacles to the eggs reaching the air freely. That's why the temple is open on three sides. We tried braving it out, assaulting the storm with missiles and projectiles. But often the eggs would be damaged, their crystalline alignments warped; and usually one farfal would get through. And one is enough to fertilize them all."

Bitterly, Nika said, "And when we've danced on the ropes, and given you your priceless eggs—what then? Do we die? One day, do we fall off? Do we slip?"

"Accidents are common. I won't lie to you. And it is necessary to keep the number of Rax small and separated from one another, until they are needed...and now you are the only one. You see, the farfellor... *compete* with the web dancers—"

"I have to fight them off?"

Those beautiful creatures were deadly, then! They were her enemies...Exkandar was silent. "And what happens afterward ?" Nika saw that he was disturbed; she knew that there would be more, and not pleasant, information. Furiously, she turned away from him. How cleverly they had trapped her!

She looked over the precipice. Now that she knew what to look for, she could see many of the strands, silvery-white, crisscrossing one another in strange, irregular grids, stretching out to invisibility.

"I won't do it! You can't force me!"

(,'There *is* something that you love more than me!" ıliash had said.) The ropes shifted and swayed in the soundless breeze. *I want to! I want to!* her mind cried out. *I could tiptoe out, ever so lightly, I could press my feet in and spring up, high, high, high, do the triple somersault, here, hovering over the emptiness*

"Curse you, ınquestors!" she said. "You made me too well!" And she trembled with longing and revulsion. "Yes," Exkandar said.

Built on stilts over the largest lake, the House of Rax must have been able to house a hundred or more web dancers. Nika was lost in it. Even her private room was as large as a moonhopper.

She threw herself into practice, which was in a varigrav gymnasium larger than the whole show-satellite had been, with silklike strands stretched over a protective forceshield. She was too immersed to notice the empty corridors hung with imagesongs and lightmobiles, the tape libraries smelling of overscrubbed disuse. But she had time to ask questions.

To become angrier.

She needed that anger, as fuel for the web dance. She had no love, no hope. Anger was all she could dredge up from inside the great emptiness.

She learned that the Rax were cloned (in both sexes, purely a cosmetic difference) from a centuries-old blueprint tissue, and that they were released into orphanages one at a time in worlds as distant as possible from one another; that a recent radical mutation of the tissue culture had almost wrecked the system, that samples had been taken from her in her sleep to rectify and perpetrate the system. That explained partly why she was the only one there now; also, there had been a rash of accidents. The Inquest was desperate indeed.

The mountain god took its toll in human sacrifice.

She learned that replacements for her were being tracked down all over the Dispersal of Man, and that after this breeding season she would be free to leave. Not because of charity.

She would be burned out. Her empathy-circuits would be ruined. Web dancing made a ruin of the mind and the body...but they would let her go. She could be a dancer still...with a different set of memories.

They would destroy her memories completely—not just the planet, the web dancing; but everything, just in case. Yes, she would truly be free.

Or dead.

But perhaps Iliash was out there among the stars, a ghost of himself with a different personality...and Nika became angrier. *I'll dance for him!* she thought. *I'll make him see me!*

If I'm angry enough I won't be afraid In her mind she tumbled again from the rope, she heard the screaming and saw the fire flash. Iliash had told her: *Anger is good It's the next best thing to courage. But push it all inside you, coil it up so it'll rush out when you need it most.*

She tumbled in the gymnasium, too, onto the springy forceshield. *It's hopeless, I'm not ready.*

She learned that they had tried to set up a forceshield under the tamweb, but the mountain had not been fooled. It had sensed an irritation in the environment, and the ova had not come.

She became angrier.

They implanted fingerlasers on both her hands and keyed them to subvocalized syllables. Now there were sounds she could never even *think* again. For hours she danced the high ropes, flicking death at farfal-robots. She learned very fast. Of course: she was made that way.

In her room she lay and gashed the walls with the fingerlasers, and when she came back the walls would always be repaired, unblemished as before. She grew angrier then, and in between practicing she lay and brooded.

Beyond her fear of slipping, beyond the anger-she saw herself, running free on the highrope, whirling against the wind, her body a perfect song of curves and arches, a still hurricane-eye of the wild elements...

It's notjust the thought ofslipping, she told herself in the darkness before sleep. *I'm not a cog in their machinel I hate them jor making me want thiS, for manipulating me this wayl I want it to be just mel* But she had sworn never to cry again, that time so many years ago. And she had never broken that oath. So she swallowed everything and woke up knotted with anger.

A few weeks later she found a holosculpture library in a circular room where half the wall could be deopaqued to show the lake that curved and dipped so abruptly into the mountainpeaks. They were both so gray, she thought, the landscape outside and the silver walls inside. No wonder the workers wore such dazzling colors. She watched the lake; it never rippled, but cast a perfect echo of the gray sky.

I'm almost angry enough-

A worker, in crimson—and-blue swirled tunic, was waiting deferentially. "May I help you, little miss? I am Ynnither, librarian of the House of Rax. The computer indicated you were here."

Nika was annoyed that her solitude had been broken so callously. "I have to be alone! I'm going to break my skull on the rocks, for the sake of the universe or something, and I can't be alone!"

"Is there something you would like to see, a particular holosculpture? Before there was so much work—"

Perhaps he could tell her something. "What about *before?* You have holosculptures of the others, of the Rax before me? Of a Rax named Iliash?" For a moment she panicked, dreading what the answer might be.

There was a rumble

"There now, miss, that'll be the big one calling for his mate," said the worker. "It'll be your time soon."

"...Iliash?" She was adamant. Ynnither said, "I remember him all right. He was the daringest of them all. To the last he was daring. Cocky. A legend to us."

"Show me."

Nika heard the hum of machinery, and the view-walls opaqued. He appeared in midair, about a meter from her face, suspended in midleap. His hair floated above him, caught in that moment. She walked closer to the holosculpture, ran her hand through emptiness. How she longed to be part of that frozen moment...

The gray eyes looked back, full of defiance.

"We have the sculpture in kinetic, too, miss," said the worker, and turned to adjust the machinery.

All at once Iliash finished his leap, in the middle of the emptiness, in one impetuous curve. Nika thought, *Not as refined as I would be. But how achingly beautiful!*

He vanished, leaped again, vanished, leaped again —with the playback in the kinetic mode, there was wind in the picture, ruffling the waves of hair; and as he landed the face broke into a smile at once triumphant and fragile.

"He was your friend, miss?" *llils?* Realization shot through her, and she felt outrage...outrage...

"He was the greatest web dancer we have had. You should have seen him in life! We often watched on the monitors in the eggroom. He's dead now."

She stared at the leaping figure till her eyes burned.

"A farfal got him, miss, on the very day he was scheduled to return to his homeworld. He needn't have danced the web that day; they'd told him it was enough. But he was wilder than usual, ran like an animal across the ropes-how we mere mortals envy your powers!—and then he shouted, *I'm going to try jor that triple somersault!'* And he stood on the rope and steadied himself for a tremendous leap. The farfal swooped down and dislodged him. They never found all the pieces."

So you're dead! she thought. Blood was on her hands and she realized how hard she had clenched them. *Control your anger, roll it into a secret place inside you so you can throw it into your leap-*

And Nika knew that she was ready. The rage had built up inside and was ready to explode. The void inside her was full.

The rumbling came again, and Exkandar was standing beside her. "You must come now, Nika. The mountain is calling for you..."

In the back of her mind she felt an alien presence, tugging at her, hungry and passionate. She did not have to be told what it was. She had been bred for empathy with aliens' minds. It was the call of the tam-creature to all the farfellor. Then they deopaqued the wall and she saw the mountain peaks jutting out over the lakeface, and her heart gave a funny leap and she let out a cry. And understood the ugly, dissonant rumbling...it was a song!

And she felt tears rushing. Choking them back, she said, "I can't help what I am, after all. Even after what you did to Iliash, the only person I've ever loved, and the others."

"Come!"

"Did you think this would make me feel like a superhero in a kid's holoplay, rushing in to save the Galaxy from the evil aliens?" she said, exulting. "I'll dance the webs—but not for your precious ships. I'll dance for Iliash, who died for my somersault. I'll dance for the perfect leap! I'll dance for ME!" And she was proud of what she was, and of her importance.

And she looked the Inquestor—a Lord of the Dispersal-full in the face, and saw...humility. And pitied him at last. The rumbling called her, thrilling her. She saw flocks of farfellor, responding likewise, flashing across the sky.

And, against the mountain peaks and the steel sky, the ghost of the boyfigure with the bright gray eyes tumbled and leaped, tumbled and leaped, over and over, with consummate grace.

After about twenty meters Nika opened her eyes.

She had been testing the web's tautness. With every cautious step she had felt the strand bend itself, accommodate itself to her weight. It was a thing alive, that strand. Not like the lifeless ropes of the show-satellite, which her own body gave life to. Here was a rope she was almost in communion with...but she did not trust it, not quite yet.

She looked. Below was Exkandar on his floater: if she tumbled, he would catch her if he could. There were other webstrands, their ends lost in the grayness. The grayness was overpowering. Space and distance were swallowed up by it, so that she seemed suspended in midnothingness.

Love me. Love me. Leap for me. Dance for me.

It was a voice not quite sentient that sang in the back of her mind, more the voice of an animal in need, broadcasting distress signals. "You poor mountain," Nika whispered. "You're just a pawn in their game, like me. Yes, I'll dance for you..."

She took a tentative leap forward, landed lightly on her right foot, spun around.

Love me more! More!

The voice tugged at her, yearned for her...she whirled once, twice, each time leaning harder into the silkstrand, catching herself miraculously just at the instant she would have tumbled.

"That's right, Nika, slowly, cautiously," prompted Exkandar's voice, reaching her via a head implant. She shrugged the voice off contemptuously. They didn't know anything, these people who used the tam-creature's eggs to control the Galaxy. Right now there was only her and the mountain, alone together.

A light wind sprang up. She took four more steps, then narrowly avoided a tumble, overcompensated for the wind, almost tripped again, flung out her arms wildly and steadied herself in a moment. Above the rumble came a high whistling, mixing with the wind sounds.

She looked up, pushing down harder with her toes and keeping her arms outstretched for the balance. A flock of farfellor broke through the cloudveils, a dozen or more of them, swooping, converging on her

Mustn't panic

(She remembered the rope slipping from under her over and over but the whisper of the mountain touched her, calmed her...)

Dance more, dance more, why do you stop?

The fighter convoy moved in to cut them off. About fifty meters above her head, a projectile volley exploded the flock into wild flurries of color. The farfellor screamed, a heartrending highpitched keening that became part of the whistling wind. *poor creatures,* Nika thought for a moment. *Sacrifices.*

But I'm going to ignore Exkandar and the farfellor and the Inquest and the fate ifthe Galaxy now. I'm just going to leap high, leap perfect, leap, she thought.

Leap for me, love me!

Impetuously, she cartwheeled across to the next strand, ran swiftly along it, leaping back to the first strand, making singing arcs in the air.

("For the sake of all of us, play it safe, girl!" she heard Exkandar say. And laughed at him...)

One of the farfellor had not been killed. It hovered over her, vulturelike, waiting. Nika ignored it, until it swooped down and knocked against her face. Angrily she whirled round and bisected it with her fingerlasers, watching the iridescent pieces fall forever into grayness...She turned back to the web dancing, feeling the pull of the mountain, *lOving* the mountain.

Suddenly the sky was alive with the flapping of farfal wings! A sea of colors crashed across the sky, and the convoys were everywhere, slaughtering. Farfal bodies plummeted like rain. Projectiles zinged and boomed.

Nika closed her eyes, reaching for the strands with her nerves, with her mind-

And leaped up, somersaulting! In her mind's eye Iliash turned with her. Her feet touched the strand and she steadied herself with relief. She laughed again, feeling the mountain's joyous response. And whirled again, arms out, like a top, with the wind flushing her face and her hair flying.

I think I can do it-

A shudder went through her, a release of rapture, thrilling her....

The mountain was giving birth! She knew it, she could feel with it, she could feel the eggs falling down the long tunnels toward the foot of the mountains.

"You've done it!" Exkandar cried. "We'll come and get you now—"

"No!" she cried. "I think I can do it."

"Do what?" She saw the floater climbing up after her. She ran along the web, farther out into the emptiness, using the bounce of the web to propel her even faster...

And then, in a moment when she found herself quite alone, she wound up all her anger and all her love, everything that was ever pent up in her slight body, and *compressed* it into a core of neutronium and then exploded, hurled herself upward-

Iliash! lliu should see me now!

—defying the planet's pull, higher than she could have thought possible, and somersaulted, with the world and the farfel colors kaleidoscoping about her eyes and the windstream burning her

One-

Two

Three-

And touched the web, giddy with triumph and joy. " .. all right," Exkandar's voice was saying. "Don't move, we'll come for you. It was a fantastic crop. You've done well by the Galaxy..."

She laughed again, a peal of laughter that scorned Exkandar and all his kind. "I've done well by me!" she shouted, her face flushed. "I've done the first triple somersault on a rope *ever!* I've danced free under the open sky with the wind singing and the mountain loving me. And I'll never forget this! I'll show you! You can erase my memory, you can discard me like another used-up tool, but I won't forget! Not ever, not if I live a thousand years!

She had come to the arena again, a grown woman still shaped like a girl, to dance the rope dance. It was the Highfest of Vangyvel—which, they had told her, was once her homeworld—and it was the nameday of the Kingling Exkandar, who would actually deign to attend. But this meant nothing to her. She stepped onto the slackrope.

There was no forceshield. She despised safety...The tiers of crowd rose to the roof of the dome. In a breath darkness fell, and she was alone in a pool of light.

She danced. She danced with a kind of crazy joy, a wildness that always drove her audience to a frenzy. But all this was routine; the climax was yet to come.

She did some dazzling footwhirls; and then, suspended only by her feet, twisted her body up the length of the rope, accelerating to the music. The crowd was deafening now, the waves of sound egging her on, pounding at her...

And then she stood in the middle of the nothingness, prevented by a thread from abrupt death. She stood frozen for a long while, while the crowd grew silent, pondering.

Her eyes fell on the royal pew, and met the eyes of Kingling Exkandar, aloof, his Inquestral shimercloak topped by the iridium crown.

Odd, she thought, *that face...*

And she closed her eyes in the ritual of the triple somersault, imagining herself away, far away, on some made-up, impossible planet:

Gray lakes, still as mirrors...

Colors, sluidng the gray sky, threatening .

Wind, caressing her...

Mountain peaks, jutting from a too-near horizon (What was the memory? From what scene in her sketchy past had it come? It would always come to her before the great leap. She seemed to remember that once, ages ago, she had filled the void inside her with anger, not love...)

And she pressed her body like an arrow into the bowstring and sprang upward, as the wind whistled and the creatures like butterflies flashed against the alien sky-

She landed. The crowd's silence broke into thunder. The strange planet retreated into her unconscious. She had been perfect.

Perfect!

As she looked out at the crowd, only a trace of the phantom memory lingered, a voice not human, crying out for her compassion-

Love me. Dance for me. Leap for me. Love me.

Frequently Asked Questions about the Inquestral Highspeech — Part III

by Professor Schnau-en-Jip

Can you tell us more about those crazy Inquestral verbs?

DEPRECATIVE STEM

Another important set of verb stems is unleased when we consider the *second umlauted* verb. This distorts the primary vowel of the verb and has a variety of inferences.

In the first instance, a second umlauted verb can be used with the particle *tyi* or *yng* and its meaning immediately becomes depreciative or abusive.

mãzhis	you are eating
tyi mẽzhis	
yng mẽzhis	you(extremely perjorative) are eating

These forms do not exist in the 1st person sing, dual, or plural. In other words, they may not be used to deprecate oneself (unless ironically by talking to oneself in the second person). The form evolved from an earlier state of the language in which strong verbs habitually used the 2nd umlaut in the second and third person singular (a similar phenomenon is found in Germanic languages on earth, cf German *ich gebe, du gibst*). In High Inquestral, strong *and* weak verbs may be subjected to this transformation, but it retains a sense of "nonce-conjugation" about it, and numerous varieties can be found. The forms are almost never found in poetry, but occasionally in transcribed *makrúgh* texts where an Inquestor elegantly insults another.

If the stem is *already* using the second umlaut form, such as with a reduplicated stem, the conjugation pushes the vowel into the rare *third umlaut stem*.

tyi memīzhis   You cretin! You've eaten already!

(implying — *how dare you eat before you are supposed to*, or some such breach of etiquette.)

If the particle *tyi* is omitted, the verb must be followed by the suffix -*kha*.

It is difficult to convey just how insulting this verb form is. Addressing an Inquestor with this verb form would probably entail immediate devivement by the nearest childsoldier on duty; however, few games of *makrúgh* are complete without at least one such use of the deprecative verb stem.

FUTURE OF VOLITION

To add *intent* to a future statement, the particle *sha* may be used with the sigmatic stem and the future endings, both active and passive.

sha shẽssio   I *will* sing! (i.e. I *demand* to sing.)
sha dhãssíver   I *will* die! (i.e. you can't stop me.)

Lettercolumn
remarks from our readers...

Write to **inquestortales@bangkokopera.com**

Two letters from "Quatermass"

I just finished Valentine this morning. Along with your signature on the title page, the facing page - under 'Also By S.P.S' - lists a collection "A Certain Slant of "I"". Is this an abandoned project or something which appeared under another title?

Here's the deal. This was supposed to be a collection of my essays from "Fantasy Review" and other sources which were very entertaining back in the 1980s and 1990s. The publisher would have been Wildside Press. Somehow this never came together but I'll put it out from Diplodocus myself sometime, as soon as I can the columns OCR'd properly.

Like MY COLD MAD FATHER, the book promised by Pulphouse Press 20 years ago, it will come out eventually, though I have to do it myself.

— Somtow

I am a fourth of the way through "Forest of the Night" aka "Riverrun II: Armorica". A 30 year old question: Was "Cruise Eternity" an except from Riverrun or its own thing?

Actually "Cruise Eternity" is its own thing. Originally written as a film treatment actually, but sat around until I turned it into a novelette.

— Somtow

From (Indecipherable)

Dear Somtow, it looks like the fifth Inquestor book is winding its way to an end. Will this also mean the end of the *Inquestor Tales* serialization?

No. I'm going to keep going because Sajit's story doesn't seem to be over yet. Also, I keep digging up the old magazine versions of the stories, and I have a whole novel about Lady Varuneh up my sleeve. I might also use it as a forum for new short stories.

— Somtow

Dear Friends:

I left America over two decades ago in order to return to my youthful vision of creating an opera company and starting a "musical revolution". I thought my literary career was behind me, but gradually I noticed that there were still people who wanted me to pick up loose ends from my novels of the 1980s or continue with the horror stories of the 1990s.

This is why, by fits and starts, I've crawled back into the world of science fiction.

But since the publishing industry has morphed into something completely new, I'm wholly dependent on my loyal readers to keep going. So, if you have a moment, go to patreon.com/spsomtow and pledge as little as $2, or as much as you feel like, and my writing career will go on as long as I get enough support from all of you.

— Somtow

The Inquestor Series

The Novels

Light on the Sound (1982)
The Throne of Madness (1983)
Utopia Hunters (1984)
The Darkling Wind (1985)

Homeworld of the Heart (in process)
   Part One: The Singing Moons (2018)
   Part Two: A Woman Cloaked in Shadow (2018)
   Part Three: The Child Collector (2019)
   Part Four: The Space Between Spaces (2020)
   Part Five: in process

in process
Vara's World

The Short Stories

The Thirteenth Utopia (Analog, 1979)
The Web Dancer (IASFM, 1979)
Darktouch (IASFM, 1980) (non-canonical)
Light on the Sound (IASFM, 1980)
The Rainbow King (IASFM, 1981)
The Dust (IASFM, 1981)
Remembrances (IASFM, 1982)
Scarlet Snow (IASFM, 1982)
The Comet that Cried for its Mother (Amazing, 1984)

www.ingramcontent.com/pod-product-compliance
Lightning Source LLC
Chambersburg PA
CBHW030257130626
46549CB00002B/578